I KEPT A TROSHIN

BY

JIMMY NICHOLSON

Happy 57th Birthday Roy.

Jimmy Nicholson.

First Published 1989
Reprinted 1993

By the same author:

More Muck Than Money

ISBN 0 9515578 0 7

Published by
S. J. Nicholson
Staithe Farm, Catfield
Great Yarmouth, Norfolk

Originally printed in England by
H. G. Stone & Co. (Printers) Ltd.
9–11 Town Green, Wymondham
Norfolk NR18 0PR

Reprinted by
Geo. R. Reeve Ltd.
Damgate, Wymondham
Norfolk NR18 0BD

CONTENTS

FOREWORD

Jimmy Nicholson's book is a delight. It spans the momentous years of two world wars, of horse drawn carriage to space exploration, of immense social change.

It is not about world events, prime ministers nor kings and queens. It traces, with a becoming honesty and openness, a lifetime within the everyday simplicity and hardship of rural life. It explores the striving from what, today, would be called poverty, to successful businessman. There are thoughts and feelings of boyhood through to husband and family man; from the early love of things mechanical to the growth of a respected and successful company.

The collection of photographs is impressive, and will have a widespread interest, but it is the word pictures, painted with a simple naivity that, for me, create the real beauty of this book. They have the impact of reality, drawing the reader into the classroom, the workplace, the storm at East Ruston and the social setting of a bygone age.

It is a book of immense general interest but it is equally a book for the connoisseur of steam. The author's lifetime involvement and experience leaps from both photograph and text. Only those with a knowledge of these mechanical giants will fully recognise the meaning of "Burrell Princess Mary", or of "Garrett", of a "Set of gallopers" or of "lugs and glands".

Perhaps, most of all, it is about the strength of character, of determination and a joy of life that shines through the reality of hardship. It draws lessons for those of us who live in the very different electronic world of today, whilst reviving memories for the contemporaries of Jimmy's boyhood.

R. D. Turley O.B.E.
HEADMASTER, STALHAM HIGH SCHOOL.

INTRODUCTION

I was prompted to write my memories of by gone days by some of my friends who have had the time and patience to listen to some of my tales about my throshin days. Some of them are amusing others I wouldn't dare write about. I only wish some of the men involved were here to read them but alas the majority are gone.

This is not the story of my life but just a few memories of the good old bad old days.

I would like to thank everybody who lent me photographs also Dr. Edmonds who reproduced them for me. Last and by no means least my daughter Carol who did all the typing.

S.J.N.

The thatched house on Church Road, Sutton where I was born with me standing in the garden. Photo taken recently by permission of present owners.

CHAPTER ONE

EARLY DAYS

THE EARLIEST memories I have of my childhood days arc looking out of the bedroom window of the house where I was born. It is a very old thatched roof place still there on Church Road, Sutton near Stalham. I can remember seeing an engine standing there I could not have been more than three years of age.

I was born on the 5th July. What a scandal it must have caused in a small village like Sutton with a population of about three hundred and fifty people, because my mother was a young girl of seventeen, daughter of a Chapel preacher and organist at Chapel. I bet some of the old dears in the village had a hey day. My mother married two years later but I kept living with my grand parents, as soon as I could I was on them engines. I was told that when I was about three years old I somehow climbed on top of an engine that stood in the yard with steam on and opened the throttle, luckily the reversing lever was in middle snotch also the engine was on top dead centre so nothing happened. If it had started up I would have been killed. I have heard Grandfather say he got up into the tender and lifted me out of the crank pit where I was standing, he hadn't seen me up there he heard it hiss when I pushed the lever. It was a 8 h.p. Marshall which Grand father had hired from a Mr Alfred Bristow who owned Stalham Flour Mill because two of his engines were commandeered for the Army. Two of my Uncles were away driving these engines. One was baling hay, the othere was carting bales to the Railway Station where it was taken to the docks and shipped to France for the horses which the soldiers were using pulling guns etc.

I was a handful for my Grandmother they tell me, I used to climb like a monkey. I was sitting on top of a straw pitcher one day when Mr Bristow came in the yard he said to Grandfather aren't you afraid to have that child up there. He said, I would rather trust him up there than I would you. I can imagine Grandfather saying that because he was very abrupt sometimes.

When I was four years old they moved house, the old thatched house with the engine yard was rented property, I have heard Grandfather could have bought it for £100.00. He thought it too much. It was for sale recently for over £90,000.

We moved to a place near Catfield Railway Station about three acres of land living accommodation was two railway carriages. One stood at right angles with the other with a sort of hut for a kitchen in the corner. I can remember Grandfather pulling one carriage round with his engine so they were side by side. They built a roof over the lot so there was space enough in the middle for two rooms. No heating was installed in the place except a small cooking stove in the kitchen, they wouldn't have got permission to build such a place today.

We lived one side and one of my uncles lived next door. It never was a very nice place to live, in the kitchen it got warm if we had a good fire but if a door was opened it soon cooled things down.

I was only four years of age when Grandfather first took me with him threshing. He travelled to work with a pony and cart and I used to ride in the cart wrapped up in a chaff bag. When we got to the engine I would sit there until he got the fire going them he would get me out and put me in the tender in the warm. He would hold me up sometimes so I could get hold of the starting lever, I soon got to know how to start the engine. As time went on and I got a little bigger I would get onto the counter shaft I could reach the lever then.

My Grandfather was in company with a farmer named John Wiseman so they traded as Wiseman and Nicholson. I had four Uncles Ted, Billy, Albert and Charlie, they were all engine drivers. Charlie the youngest, had an accident he lost a finger in the riddle wheel on the drum, he got back to work stunted his thumb on the same hand so he finished up having the thumb off. He got some compensation money, I think some of this money was used to buy these railway carriages and the land.

In 1921 the Company was split up, I can just remember the auction which was held on a little meadow in Sutton. Houses are built there now. Grandfather let me start his engine at the sale, Jonathan Howlett, the auctioneer, said he would sell the driver with the engine, it was the usual thing to run the turnout at a sale.

Before I started weekday school I went to Sunday School which started at 10 a.m. on Sunday morning, finished at 11 a.m. then into Chapel for another hour then walk home for dinner which didn't amount to much as nothing was done on a Sunday in the way of cooking, then back to school at 1.30 p.m. another hour in there then back into Chapel for another service, out at 3.30 p.m. home to tea, sometimes the Preacher came to tea. After tea it was back to Chapel again at 6.30 p.m. out at 7.30 p.m. if you were lucky because one of the older members were quite likely to start a prayer meeting and they would all be praying away for another half hour or so, I couldn't make it all out at the time.

I know Grandfather would have liked me to have grown up to be a Chapel preacher, but as I grew older I began to get other ideas but I have some good memories of those days. Every year in May or June we had our Sunday School Anniversary, a platform would be put up around the pulpit big enough to hold the children, teachers and helpers. The front of the platform had an ornamental rail all decked out with flowers, the whole place was trimmed up with lilac etc. When I see lilac now it always reminds me of Sutton Anniversary, we would sing special hymns written for the big day, say recitations and dialogues some would sing a solo. It was a big occasion the Chapel and Schoolroom was full, the collection for the day was about £11.00.

Grandfather's brother Albert was Sunday School Superintendant, in fact he organised everything at Chapel. He was also an engine driver.

On Ingham Fair Monday, which was a week after Whitsun, we would have a trip to the seaside, all the teachers and children would be loaded onto wagons which were pulled by a traction engine, it was then Eccles beach here we come. I can remember seeing four engines standing there all had loads of children from different Sunday Schools from the surrounding villages.

Using engines for this job came to an end when the law came out that to do haulage work they had to be licensed the same as a lorry which was much more expensive. So after that we

This is the first 8 h.p. Garrett that Grandfather had, taking a party from Lessingham to Bacton Beach about 1908. She was named 'Alice'

had horses and wagons. The horses were lent with their team-man from local farmers. The horses were trimmed up with their best harness with brasses on and ribbons.

After having lots of fun on the beach we would get back to the Chapel for tea which some of the ladies had prepared. After tea we would all go to a meadow and play games, run races etc. We would all go home tired out.

At Christmas we always had a party in the schoolroom, plenty of food to eat and every child had a present. Also every child had a prize book. A special book was given to the child who had the best attendance in each class. What amazes me when I think about it is how this was all paid for because the only money they had was the £11.00 from the Anniversary and a few pounds collected from Carol singing at Christmas.

One of the old ladies, who was a teacher, was a spinster, she didn't like children a lot she was always telling us boys off, we would tease her and she would get upset. Once when we were having a tea party the cups and plates were in a big linen basket, Sophie was her name, she fell backwards on top of the crockery ware and laid there with her legs in the air, she had to be pulled out.

Another old dear who was Chapel cleaner liked us kids even less than Sophie did, we used to call her 'miser' she was a funny one—when it was proposed to have electric light in the Chapel she said she didn't want anything to do with the stinking old gas lamps. I think she liked the new lights they were easier to keep clean. Also easier to light once she got the knack of switching them on.

This was taken in the yard behind the thatched house at Sutton about the turn of the century, the three boys on the Holmes Engine are my uncles.

CHAPTER TWO

SCHOOL DAYS IN THE TWENTIES

AT THE age of five, of course, I had to start school for real which I didn't think much of. I never was a brilliant scholar but there were some there worse then me. I was never really interested, I think if I had tried a bit more on some subjects I could have done better. All I wanted to do was get up onto them engines. If I heard one working I would be gone. I used to get wrong, sometimes the cane, because of this habit.

The School Mistress was a very strict lady her home was London, she lodged in the village with Mr & Mrs Miles who lived in Moor Road. She was also very much Church of England she had no time at all for children that attended Chapel, so as my family were very much Chapel I was never very popular, in fact I could never do anything right. The good lady's name was Miss Mary Landon. When she was angry her face would turn blue. She had a weapon about fifteen inches long and about an inch thick and she knew how to use it if we did anything wrong.

The School itself stands next to the Church, it always seemed a miserable sort of place, it had two rooms one was for the infants the big room was for the eight years of age and over, the colour scheme always was the same, dark green at the bottom light green at the top with a darker line in the middle.

The lighting was from parafin lamps hanging from the ceiling on chains. The only form of heating in the place was from a coal fire in the big room and a very small coal fire in one corner in the infants room. The only people who got any benefit from them were the teachers who in cold weather always seemed to be standing in front of them. If it was frosty the water would be running down the walls.

There was no drinking water on the place, there was a pump in the infants and girls porch cum cloakroom but it never worked. If we wanted a drink we always went to the cottages opposite, there were two big barrells which held soft water from the roof which had taps in the bottom. Those taps were sometimes turned on just as we went into the classroom so the water would run out, but nobody ever knew who did it. The toilets were in a row behind the school, boys one end the girls and infants the other end, also there was a special one for the teachers, they all had little doors at the back.

On the gable end of the School there was a bell which was rung every morning at five minutes to nine, I had to take a turn in the mornings pulling a rope which rang it. We would make the Head Mistress very angry by throwing stones up and hitting the bell which made it

School group taken about 1927. Miss Landen on the left, my friend Bob Baker on the back row far right, I am third from right back row.

ring. I have been kept in after all the others had gone home many a time and made to write one hundred lines 'I must not stone the bell'. I could write that with my eyes shut I got so used to the job.

Another lad who lived near us started school the same day as I did we became friends and carried on being friends until he died at the age of forty nine. His name was Bob Baker, his father was a builder. Both of us were copped one day stoning the bell so we both had to stay in. As we were writing our lines Bob had wind I laughed and got a clip round the ear hole. When we eventually got out we picked up some more stones and let the old bell have another dose, we dived over the bank into the Church yard when we peeped over the bank Miss Landon was standing on the step looking round, of course she couldn't see us. I remember her face was blue with temper. She hadn't enough evidence to punish us again but I am sure she had a good idea who did it.

Another time I remember having to stay in I was sitting well back in the class I had my eye on Mary, when she wasn't looking I moved up a bit nearer the door, the next move was a dash for the exit but my jacket pocket hooked the end of a desk I kept going pulled the desk round and took the pocket clean off, I didn't half cop it when I got home. The next afternoon I was made to stay in again and write more lines.

I was about twelve years old when Miss Landon retired, she was Head Mistress there for thirty six years. She taught my mother when she was at school. Everyone at Sutton said what a good teacher she was but she didn't have one pupil pass the Scholarship in all those years. She bought every child in the School a book when she retired, I remember mine was about engines.

One of the vicar's daughters came as Head Teacher, she didn't last long, we were a bit too much for her. I would make a noise like an engine threshing another boy who in later years worked for me would hum like a drum, between us we nearly crazed her. She would sit on a desk and cry. After she left another one of her sisters came, she was a bit tougher, a bang over the head was her way of saying no. I don't think it did us any harm.

In those days the dentist would come round the schools with a horse drawn caravan, all his instruments were pedal power. One day an inspector came. I didn't like them, they didn't seem to understand us country boys. Anyway, he squared us all up after looking at some of the work and made his departure. After a few minutes he was back. He asked the teacher if some boy could help him as he had a flat tyre. Of course I was picked to do the job, it was right up my street. When I got to the car I asked him if he had a jack to lift the car up. He didn't seem to know, but I found one in the back. It was a Bull Nose Morris with only three wheel studs. I found the wheel brace and started to loosen the nuts. He said one side goes one way and the other side is different, I knew he hadn't much idea what he was talking about. I said I know which way they go. How do you know he asked. I said I live on bolts and nuts. After the job was done he gave me sixpence. He went into school and said to the teacher, that boy know what he's doing. She said, oh, I'm glad he knows something.

Bob Baker, my mate, and myself had a lot of fun after school hours playing with our hoops which were bowled along the road with a stick. I can remember running my hoop into the front wheel of some fellows bicycle, he went over the handlebars onto the road he got up and chased me, he didn't catch me. I was a good runner, he was swearing he picked up my hoop which was a metal one and gave it a fling it landed on top of a telephone pole. I remember getting a long piece of wood and getting the hoop down.

Then there was the spinning top season. We used to spin them with a whip home made from a straight stick and a leather boot lace. When we hit the top it would crack and sometimes fly high in the air, but it was still spinning when it came down.

Then there were marbles to play, sometimes we had some glass ones with coloured stripes in. One Saturday morning my Grandmother told me to walk to Stalham, which was two miles, and get her somethings from Hensmans Stores I can't remember exactly what I had to get but I do remember she wanted some peppermint sweets, also she handed me a letter to post on the way there.

When I got in Sutton Street I met two of my school chums so I arranged for them to come with me. I got to the stores and did the shopping all right I then went to another shop and bought some marbles. We then started playing with these marbles, I think the other boys had some with them so we had a lovely time. Instead of arriving home at dinner time it was well into the afternoon. I had the peppermints mixed up with marbles and the letter still in my pocket. Grandmother wer'nt half angry. She grabbed the broom, which stood handy, and set about me. I remember running away from her, that took a long time to live down.

The local chimney sweep lived in a cottage opposite the school his name was Joe Adams, he had a horse and trap. A trap was a little cart with seats each side with a little door at the back. He used this outfit to get about his sweeping job. In the summer he would turn his horse out to grass on a field joining the churchyard, part of this field was excavated for sand and gravel, it was called the gravel hole. There was a foot path through this field into the churchyard, it was a short cut to the school. Us lads would ride Joe's horse bareback round the field until one day Joe caught us. He came and saw my Grandfather and told him I was the ring leader. I was told off and threatened with a good hiding if it happened again.

When I was eleven years old I went threshing during the school holidays. I was chaff sacker and did this every holiday time earning enough money to buy all my own clothes.

I had a day off school and went with Grandfather to the Royal Norfolk Show which was held on the meadows at Crown Point at Trowse. It was the first show I had been to so I was very excited seeing all those brand new engines and drums lined up. There were Burrells, Garretts, Marshall, Ruston, Ransome, Clayton and Wallace. Also new chaffcutters and straw pitchers; there was also the horses, pigs and cattle to look at. I remember seeing the Prince of Wales there. Mr Ballam, Home Sales Manager, for Garretts of Leiston, lifted me up so I could see him go passed in an open top car. I was not all that big but I thought he didn't look much bigger than I was. I think it was 1924.

When I was sacking chaff Grandfather would sometimes do the job and let me look after 'Totty' that was the name of his engine which I could drive by the time I was about ten years old.

When I was thirteen I was helping Uncle Ted threshing at Stalham he was short of a drum feeder so I drove his engine while he did the feeding. I did this for a week, we were threshing off the shock. He got fixed up with another man who did the feeding so I went back to chaff sacking. The last day I should have been at school I didn't go because Grandfather and two of my Uncles took an engine to Loddon. One they had overhauled for Mr Cooper, a farmer who was also a relative of ours so I ask if I could go with them, Grandfather said I could so at half past two in the morning away we go towing Ted's motor bike and sidecar behind. We made an early start so we could get through Norwich before the trams started at six o'clock, but didn't quite make it. When we were going through Magdalen Street Ted was driving and got wedged beside a tram, I can still see him backing the engine a bit so they could get passed. We had to push the motor bike back. I can remember people laughing and pointing at us when we were going up Tombland, there was, Grandfather on the bike me on the pillion behind. I should think it must have been a sight worth seeing. We arrived at Loddon about dinner time. Ted and Charlie came home on the motor bike. Grandfather and myself were brought back to Norwich by Mr Cooper's son in a car. We then caught a bus to Stalham then walked the two miles home to Sutton. It was a fair old day for a fourteen year old.

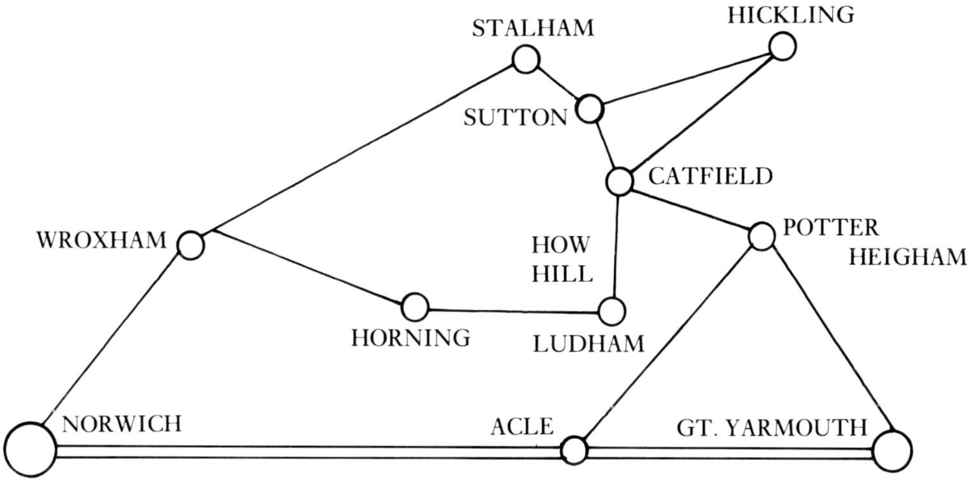

East Norfolk.

This is the engine I had a lucky escape on at the age of three.

CHAPTER THREE

GRANDPARENTS AND RELATIONS

MY GRANDFATHER was born at Upton and brought up at Acle. He told me he left school when he was eleven years of age. His elder brother Tom lived at Caister-on-Sea, I think some of his descendents still live around there. Tom was an engine driver as was his younger brother Albert who lived on Stalham Green. Albert drove for Gladden and Co., of Ingham near Stalham. Their father Jesse Nicholson was also an engine driver, he was my Great Grandfather. My Great Great Grandfather owned two threshing drums which were worked by horses they walked round in the farmyard turning a big gear wheel which in turn worked a driving shaft coupled to the drum shaft. This was before steam was used. The drums were only small machines which had taken the place of the frail.

Grandfather told me his father said, sometimes when they got to work in the morning they found someone had been there in the night and smashed the big cast iron gear wheel. These people didn't like the threshing drum, they thought it would do them out of a job. The frail was a thing hinged in the middle which they used to knock the corn out and these people who used these frails could see that the drum would put an end to that. At that time they had a farm at Salhouse.

When my son Malcolm came with me threshing he made the sixth generation of Nicholsons to do that job. But I find I still don't know so much about engines as some of these enthusiasts do.

When Grandfather left school his first job was driving the steam engine in Fishley Mill which drove a water wheel to pump water from the marsh dykes into the river. When he was fourteen he took a threshing set which his elder brother had been driving. Of course in those days it was a Portable Engine which had to be moved from farm to farm with horses. I think all the family worked for some people at Acle by the name of Squires who were farmers, they also owned four sets of threshing tackle. All the engines and drums were built by Holmes of Norwich.

He then moved to Martham and took charge of a traction engine and drum for a Mr Cross who had two sets, both of which were Burrells built at Thetford. After a while he came to Sutton and drove for Mr Tom Worts of Mill Farm. It was a new outfit built by Marshall of Gainsborough. He lodged at the White Horse public house which was opposite the church. This pub has been closed for many years, I don't remember it as a pub.

Grandfather told me that when he came and drove the engine for Tom Worts of Sutton the

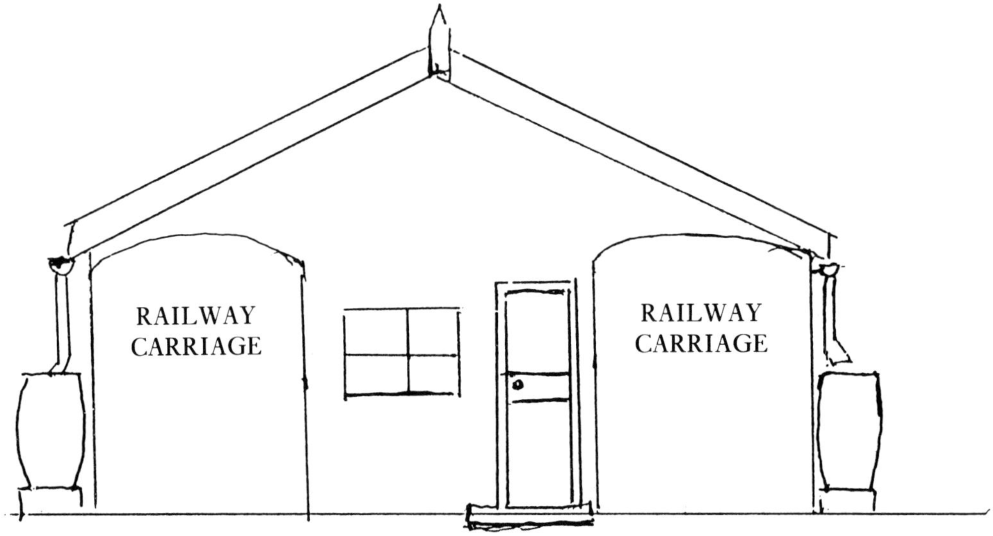

FRONT END VIEW

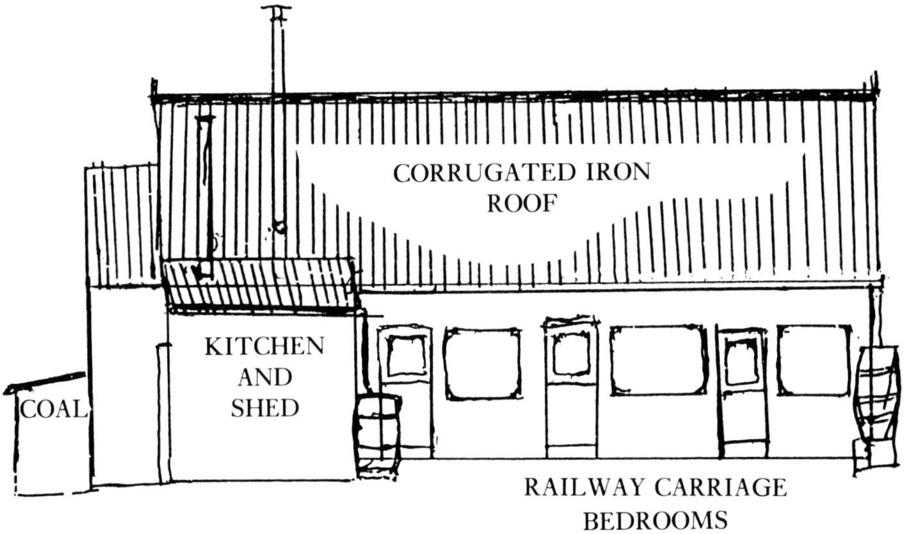

SIDE VIEW

Our house.

fellow who was his drum feeder was named Frank Ewells, he would give him a spell so he had a chance to drive while they were threshing. Anyway, this man Ewells left Sutton and went and drove an engine for a man at Easton near Norwich, he was the driver of the engine that went through Cringleford Bridge the whole turnout crashed down into the river. Both the driver and steersman were killed. I think this tragedy happened in 1901.

My Grandparents were married in 1888 at Acle, they lived in a cottage at Mill Farm, Sutton. He moved from Worts a few years later and drove for Mr Neave a farmer at East Ruston. This man bought a new engine in 1890, it was a Holmes 8 h.p. engine. Grandfather told me he unloaded it off the railway at Vauxhall Station at Great Yarmouth and took it to the South Deans to the Norfolk Showground, which was held that year at Yarmouth. He said Holmes had posters printed and put up to say theirs was the only engine to get on the showground without sinking in the sand.

When Mr Charles Lee Neave died Grandfather carried on driving for his Executors, who were Mr John Wiseman of Oby and Mr Silcock of Catfield. After a year or two Grandfather had more work then he could do so as his oldest son Ted was then sixteen they bought another new outfit, it was a Garrett outfit. So Ted drove the Holmes outfit and Grandfather took the Garrett, it was a great big ugly 8 h.p. engine. Years later I drove it for a time.

Another two years passed and the third set was bought, another 8 h.p. Garrett, brand new with drum and pitcher. Billy, the second son was nearly sixteen so he drove the Holmes. Ted took the new one, they were running three sets. In 1911 Grandfather thought he would start in business on his own so he got a little financial help and went to the Royal Show, which was held at Crown Point, Trowse and bought another new 7 h.p. Garrett with drum and pitcher, of course he took all the work he had been doing with Wiseman and Silcock, they weren't very pleased. Anyway, about three years later Wiseman asked Grandfather if he would go in company with him if he paid Silcock out. So the company Wiseman and Nicholson was formed. The old Holmes turnout was sold and another new 7 h.p. Garrett turnout was bought, Albert, the third son drove the oldest Garrett, Billy had the last new one.

I have heard some of these engine men say they didn't like a Garrett engine. Some said they wouldn't pull, I can tell them now—that is if any of them are still with us—that after my Grandfather had operated on them they would pull as good as any other make and govern on a drum perfectly. I always found them a very economical engine, I drove one for several years. Teddy Ballam, Sales Manager for Garretts, said to Grandfather, there is something about you people we can't understand.

Grandfather split his share four ways so three of the sons, all drivers had a share. By 1921 the sons were getting restless because they were doing the work and Wiseman was taking half the money, so they sold up. Grandfather, Billy and Albert bought their own turnouts at the sale with financial help from some of the local farmers. Everything made a lot of money which was not so good for them really, but it put more money in the kitty.

Ted couldn't get anyone to back him so Thurlow of Stowmarket fixed him up with a 8 h.p. Burrell engine and a new Garrett drum and straw pitcher and Clayton 5 knife cutter, all their other chaffcuters were innes of Hitchen. The engine had to go back to Burrells and have a new half barrell put on the boiler also a new cylinder block. Ted had an argument with Thurlow about the age of this Burrell engine, at the finish they took it back, it was sold to W. J. Sandell of Worstead. It is the same engine that Bunn of Great Yarmouth now own, they call it Big A.

My grandparents.

Grandfather with his engine.

Albert and Billy had bought another second-hand turnout, a 6 h.p. Garrett, also a drum and pitcher. The engine came from Cornwall, it was a nice turnout. So Ted took this turnout over after his Burrell was gone.

Charlie, the youngest son, went into partnership with Grandfather. After a few years Ted bought a single crank compound Burrell and I bought the 6 h.p. Garrett. When Grandfather retired from driving he still went around with Charlie, who was by then driving his engine, he would sack chaff, he also made a lot of cultivators for Mr Benton of Sutton, they were known as the Benton Patent Cultivator, which was a horse drawn implement for use in between rows of blackcurrant bushes. He worked until he was nearly ninety years of age, he was still smoking an ounce of tobacco a day, he was a tough old fellow and he expected everybody to be like him. He passed on when he was ninety three years old.

When I hear some of these people today running on about what we should or shouldn't eat I think of him. I have seen him eating sausage rolls with fur growing out, also rotten oranges, he would eat the peel as well. If he had shrimps he would eat the lot, shell and all.

After Grandmother died he lived on his own for thirteen years. I called to see him one day, he said he had lost his pipe, I don't know what *ira* done with it, he said, so we fixed him up with another one. I called again a few days later, he said, *ira* found my pipe, you'd never guess where it was, it was in the kittle. He had been making his tea from that kettle, that pipe was as clean as a new pin.

If he had a bad head he would gather some stinging nettles and boil them in some water, he called it nettle tea, it looked some rum stuff. He said it did him good. I never did see him wear an overcoat. I have seen him come home from threshing wet through he would sit in the little kitchen near the cooking stove with steam going away from him.

One morning he was walking to Smallburgh, he was nearly eighty years old, he was off chaff sacking with Charlie, it was a dark morning he had his frail basket on his back with his food and a bottle of cold tea in, when a car come along and knocked the old fellow down. The young man driving the car stopped and picked him up, as it happened he knew Grandfather so he said, I had better take you home Mr Nicholson, but the old boy had other ideas. I don't want to go home I am going to work, so the man gave him a lift the rest of the way. The only damage was a broken tea bottle. He worked all day went home, didn't say anything to Grandmother until a young man came to the door asking if he was all right.

He would always be singing 'I'm a pilgrim bound for Glory', it was an old Sankey hymn. I'm afraid all his efforts to keep me on the straight and narrow didn't work out as he would have liked. I think I had rather too much Chapel when I was young.

The coal man called one day. He heard Grandfather telling him how much to leave but couldn't see him at first, then he noticed him up on the roof, he was over eighty years old then. He was sweeping the chimney which had to be done from the top because it was only a six inch pipe from the cooking stove.

When he came home from work sometimes Grandmother would fry some longshore herring and boil some taters, he would say, 'we wholly live though we don't git much money', another saying of his was 'A bad workman always find fault with his tools'.

Grandmother was born at Reedham, the daughter of a pork butcher and dealer, her maiden name was Providence Mallett. For years she was the local, very often unpaid, midwife. I can remember her being called up in the night to go to some woman having a baby, I remember hearing her telling some one how many children she had helped to bring into the world, I know it was well over a hundred.

She never had many luxuries in life, Grandfather made her a washing machine, I have never seen another one like it. It was a boat shaped thing on four legs and had a pair of rollicks in the middle to put a dolly in. She had to work this thing back and forth, and would put hot water and soap in then add the linen. It got most of the muck out. She used to light a fire in the copper first, I think she would boil the dirtiest linen such as our shirts, which sometimes had plenty of grease on, we weren't so fussy in them days. We would wash our hands and face and neck outside near the back door, we would have a bowl of water on an old bench. If it was really bad weather we would get in the shed. I don't think Grandmother ever liked living in them railway carriages which we called home. It was never a good place to live the only heating we had was a cast iron cooking range with a small oven, the fire area was about eight inches square. It would get warm in the little kitchen but the rest of the place was like an ice house. The bedrooms were in the carriages, water would be dropping from the ceiling if it was frosty. I can remember in the winter I couldn't get into bed and put my feet down because the bed clothes were damp.

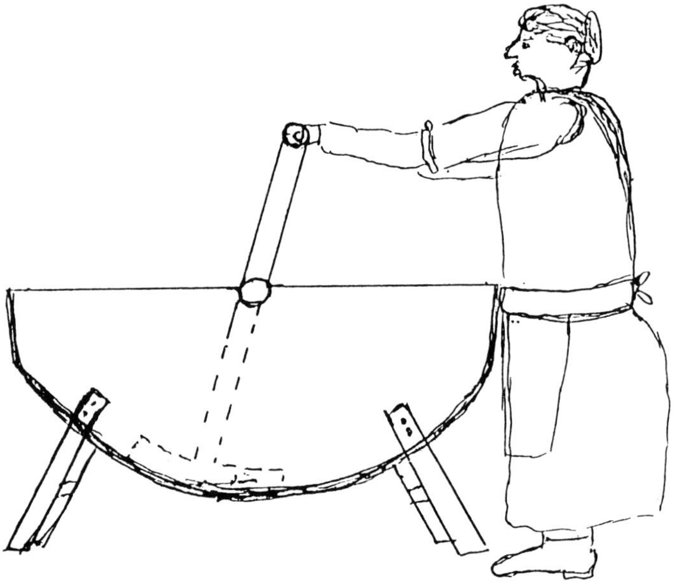

Grandmothers washing machine.

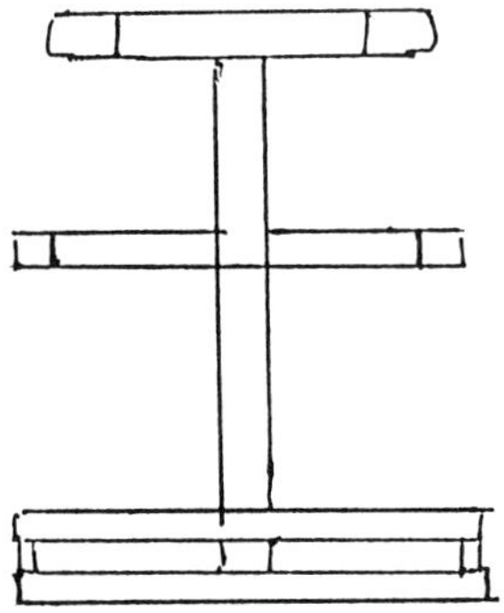

The dolly.

When we came home from work sometimes wet through there was no real means of drying our clothes properly, I have put my overalls on may a time still wet. How my Grandparents put up with that I don't know. I was glad when I married and got into a brick house. Grandmother died in 1943 aged 77 years.

Sometimes when they were working in the yard repairing the engines and drums etc ready for the next season there would be a fire on the forge in the old workshop so Grandmother would bring a saucepan full of potatoes and put on the fire to boil for dinner. Every little while the old dear would come and give the handle on the bellows a few pumps to keep the fire going. One of the men working in the yard watched his opportunity and took the spuds off and put a similar saucepan on the fire which was full of old bolts. When Grandmother thought the potatoes were cooked she lifted the lid and had a look in and realised it was not her saucepan. She didn't half carry on. You won't get any dinner today George, she said. Grandfather said, I don't know anything about it and I don't suppose Ted do either. Of course Ted was the culprit. We had to wait until the spuds were cooked. 'Happy days'.

Grandmother always packed our food up overnight as we were always away very early, I didn't have milk in my tea so in my haste one morning I took her vinegar bottle by mistake, they both looked alike as our lighting weren't too good. When I got to the engine I took the bottle out and stood it in the tender near the firebox door to warm up. When we had got going I picked the bottle up to have a swig and got a mouthful of hot vinegar. I did some spitting for a minute or two.

Grandmother always kept a few hens in the garden they would produce a few eggs, she always had a cockerel with them. One old cock bird always started to crow early in the morning if he crowed before midnight it was a sure sign of rain.

As I said before, Grandfather, Uncle Billy and Albert bought their turnouts at the auction but Ted's engine was bought by Mr H Barber, a farmer at Catfield. The drum and pitcher went away I don't know who bought them. After a few years the engine named 'Jumbo' was put down Hickling Stub Mill to drive a water pump, a shed was built over it. After Mr Barber died the engine was sold to S Witham of Erpingham who used it for threshing, after a time it was sold again. I remember going to see a man in Suffolk, in his yard stood this big 8 horse Garrett. I recognised it straight away, it was 'Jumbo', as big as ever, I think it was cut up there.

The other engines my people had all had names, there was Totty, Alice, Samson, Prince Henry, Daphny and Churchill, they were all Garretts.

The Burrell compound of Teds had a brass plate on the smokebox door 'Little Mary', funny enough his wife's name was Mary. Ted's first wife died in 1918 when there was a big outbreak of influenza, he lived with us until he remarried in 1924.

Grandfather's brother Albert, who was Great Uncle to me, drove an engine for Gladden & Co. of Ingham, it was an 8 h.p. Marshall. He drove it from new, bringing it home from the Norfolk Show, which I have been told was at Fakenham, in 1896. Uncle drove it about forty years, when he retired his son Jack drove it. She was always called the Company Engine as all the biggest customers were share holders.

After Billy went from Stalham he set up threshing at Shotesham, he had all sorts of engines there. My cousing Tom, son of Billy, drove the last genuine Savage traction engine made. Billy also had a MacLaren engine when he was at Stalham, this engine was not very economical in fact she was a coal burner. He did all sorts to her but he couldn't improve it much. This engine was bought from W B Gaze of North Walsham. When Billy first had it it wouldn't govern on the drum but he did cure that. It did improve the coal consumption a bit.

Uncle Ted chaff cutting with Jumbo the 8 h.p. Garrett at Potter Heigham.

CHAPTER FOUR

WORKING FOR REAL

HAVING FINISHED with school I started working for Grandfather with his threshing machine. He travelled to work in his horse and cart and I had to ride with him. He said to make sure I got there on time. It meant getting up about five o'clock. I soon got the job of going down the yard in the dark to the stable each morning to yoke the pony. The old horse was getting a bit slow so we had to allow plenty of time. If there was a frost so the roads were slippery we had to walk and lead the horse. One morning we were going to Barton Turf about four miles from home when all of a sudden the poor old mare slipped onto her backside, she just sat there with us still in the cart. Ralph Buckingham, our drum feeder was riding with us. Grandfather had the reins, he said 'Come on old gal git up', she managed to stand up, we thought we were away but as she stood up the belly band broke so up go the shafts and out the back we went onto the road. There were dinner bags and oil cans everywhere, me being only a boy I was a bit scared. It soon got sorted out, George, that was Grandfather's name, had some copper rivetts in his pocket so he did a quick repair job. The only lights we had were a pair of candle lamps on the cart.

She was a funny old horse she would follow that engine anywhere, I had the job of driving her, behind the turnout, when they moved I would hold her back sometimes until they got well away then let her go, she would gallop up the road like a racehorse until we got behind the strawpitcher. Sometimes she would throw a shoe off, that meant a new shoe, I remember one night I was pumping the bellows on the forge, George was fitting the shoe on one of her back feet all of a sudden she lifted her tail I shouted, look out, he dropped her foot but he weren't quick enough he stopped a big lump on the neck, I laughed but he didn't think it very funny he weren't half angry, I thought he was about to throw the hammer at me.

I had one season sacking chaff, I didn't think much of that job, it was one of the muckiest jobs on the turnout especially near the end of the season when the stacks were cut about with rats and mice. Some of the farmers would put poison in the rat holes, when they were putting that through the drum this poison would be blowing out everywhere, I can remember this stuff would make my throat sore. Not a very nice job really for a boy but I did get man's pay, six shillings and sixpence per day. Some of the farmers would moan about paying a boy man's wages but I noticed no body else wanted the job.

We only got paid when it was fine weather if it was wet or windy so we couldn't thresh we didn't get any money at all. Sometimes in the winter we would only do two days in a week, I have known some weeks when we didn't do anything. I got a bit fed up with this so I asked Grandfather if I could put a shed in his garden to do some bicycle repairs in, of course he said yes. With the little money I had saved I bought some wood and corrugated iron and built a shed so wet days I would be in my workshop earning a shilling. I sold carbide for bicycle gas lamps, 2d a tin. I also bought a treddle lathe, it cost six pounds, it was on this machine I learned lathe work which has come in very handy since.

I went with Albert sacking chaff at Martham when the farmer paid the men they asked for insurance money which was ninepence per week, he grumbled but of course he knew he had to pay as he employed them on Monday so he gave me my money last, I think we did three days, so it came to nineteen shillings and sixpence, he then gave me another ninepence, I didn't say anything I took the money but I was not old enough to have an Insurance Card. If the farmer wouldn't pay this ninepence some of the men would write their name in the place where the stamp should be. If this happened the farmer had to pay the full amount which was one shilling and sixpence, that didn't go down very well.

At the end of my first season I began to do a bit of bond cutting also I had a go at feeding the drum. Just before the next harvest Albert had an accident on his motor bike. He had one leg badly smashed up and was off work about twelve months so they had to find someone to drive his engine. Herbert Mallett a chap who had been driving for Billy took the big eight horse engine, not a very handy machine and kept Alberts work going. Ralph Buckingham who was feeding with Grandfather took the MacLaren engine for Billy so I was then feeding an sacking corn with George. It was hard work for a fifteen year old. I know I used to be tired when I got home at night I didn't want to do any jogging to get some exercise as I see some of them doing these days. My fingers used to wear through at the ends I said to Grandfather look at my fingers they are bleeding, he said, that will toughen them up. That was all the sympathy I got from him. I then made some long thimbles from tin, that saved the ends of my fingers. I used to make differant sizes and sell some to the other drum feeders who I knew, I think I got 3d each for them.

Midway through the season Ted's drum feeder left, he asked Grandfather if I could go with him, which I did. We would take turns driving and feeding, I liked driving his engine I was used to it as I had driven it several times during school holidays. It was a 6 h.p. Garrett No: 27556 I will always remember that number as I read it hundreds of times.

The first place I went with him was Laurels Farm, Ludham. We were working at the off farm which was called Manships. It was just a barn and some cottages where some of the farm hands lived. I think we did three barley stacks there, they weren't half day stacks they were some good size lumps. We were on the finish of the last one when it started raining so by the time we got packed up things were getting pretty wet and so was I. One of these men had a wife who was always hanging about there, I think she was a bit simple. They had a horse and cart loaded up with corn when they pulled away the horse went down in the mud which was pretty deep and broke both shafts off the cart. Old Mr Mattocks the boss had come to see how things were going, it was the first time I had seen him, he started swearing, he told this woman to bugger off indoors out of the way, he didn't half let rip. The next day we did a day's chaff cutting up at the farm, it was a big hay stack. They would brotch nine yards for a days cutting we didn't have any time to spare to get that lot through in time to move before it was dark. We were ready to start when Mr Mattocks came round, his men were getting the thatch off so he said something about picking the pegs up. I stood near the engine with another young fellow, we couldn't understand all he said because he was a broad Scott. We laughed, he got angry and

TOP *Ingham Mill in full sail with Grandfather's brother Albert on the 8 h.p. Marshall Engine with Holmes Drum and Elevator, in the early 1900's. This was called The Company Engine.*
BOTTOM *Cousin Tom threshing with the last Savage Engine built.*

said, 'Don't stand there laughing like a pair of ****** monkeys', what he meant was for us to pick the brotches up which wasn't our job anyway.

When we finished he gave us a shilling extra and said we had done well.

When we used steam engines we would cook herrings and kippers on a shovel full of fire, the driver would make sure he had a clear fire before we stopped for either breakfast or dinner then get the long fire shovel full and lay the fish on top. They were good food, sometimes you would bite on a cinder, but that was all part of the fun.

The next season I was back with Grandfather and Charlie, I had that season spelling over feeding the drum and sacking corn. By now I was a full blown drum feeder. I was still doing my cycle repairs on wet days and sometimes well into the night. I reached the age of sixteen so I was classed a man. I could lift a coomb of corn as good as the next one. A coomb of wheat was eighteen stone, barley sixteen, oats twelve and beans were nineteen, we didn't get too many of them. We did a little seed drawing, not much as there never was a lot of clover grown in this neck of the woods. We had pleny of chaff cutting some of the stuff we were expected to cut wasn't fit to put through a cutter. We always seem to get plenty of marsh hay sometimes we had to take the riddles out to get it through, it was so light and full of muck.

I hated cutting hay on a frosty morning, the wind out of the fan would hit you straight in the face, and we would be covered in muck, but, over the years I got used to it.

We had a young lad who was a relation to Grandmother come over from Lowestoft to work as he couldn't find any in the town. He lived with us and came sacking chaff, he was only fourteen years old.

We were threshing at Happisburgh when we stopped for dinner, George, that was his name, took a great big meat and onion roll out of his dinner tin. Grandmother made these rolls, one would be enough for dinner. The farmer's big black bitch was watching him, he said to this dog, you would like this wouldn't you, no sooner said than done, this animal grabbed his meat roll from his hand and swallowed it. When he told the farmer about it he laughed and said, you have to watch her boy she will eat anything. He didn't offer the boy anything extra when he paid him.

I was feeding the drum at East Ruston when a thunderstorm came up quick. Another young fellow, Billy Addy was his name, was cutting bonds. There was a flash of lightning and an almighty bang, the same time the air smelt of sulphur. There was an old man carting chaff with a horse and tumbril, the horse ran away and threw the poor old fellow out he finished up in the dyke. I don't think he was bady hurt but they had to take him home. All the horses were frightend, I can remember the farm men running about there catching them. It started raining and within minutes everywhere was flooded. I know we got nicely wet getting the cloth over the drum. The men who were trying to cover the stack were half drowned everyone there was scared, I know I was.

The next summer I went with Ted on his motor bike and sidecar to a sale at Bunwell. It was when the late Mr Isaac, Sheldrakes Machines were sold, I think it was 1933. He had several sets of tackle and there were quite a few spare engines. I seem to remember seeing some Savage engines there, I know there was some very old Marshalls. The best outfit was a Burrell engine with a Garrett drum and elevator, the lot was bought by Mr Bertie Shelldrake for £530. The engine was a double crank compound she was five years old. It is still around No: 4055, now named 'Crimson Lady'. I can remember seeing that engine new at the Norfolk Show in 1927.

Also at the sale was a 8 h.p. Burrell, an old engine with crossarm governers and extra wide back wheels, it was sold with a Marshall drum and pitcher. This outfit was bought by Mr Tom King of Poringland.

Just before this Billy had some trouble so he got a job driving this turnout for Tom King. He hadn't been there many weeks when he was off work from blood poison and he was really ill for a time so Tom King came over and saw Grandfather to see if somebody could drive Billy's engine. The only one he could spare was me, I was just seventeen years old. So it was arranged for me to go the next afternoon after we had finished threshing, so the next day I had to hurry home and have a wash and bike to Stalham and catch a bus to Norwich. It was a privately owned bus company then, owned by Mr Robinson later he sold out to the United Bus Company. I then caught another bus to Poringland. After walking a mile or two I found my new boss, he took me to my lodgings and told me where I would find the engine the next morning. As I had never been in charge of an engine before I was getting a bix anxious, I had done plenty of driving with someone else with me but not alone. Anyway, the next morning I was up and away I went on a borrowed bike. I could see the straw pitcher in the light of my bicycle lamp. I went into the field hoping it was the right engine, the fire was laid ready so all I had to do was put a match to it. I hadn't been there long when the drum feeder came, he said, what are you our new driver. He looked at me a bit doubtful. As we were about to start threshing the trace on the straw pitcher broke so I had to do a quick repair job. I really did think I was an engine driver then. Anyway, we got the job done the more I did the more confidence I got. I stopped with Mr King until Billy was back to work then I came home again to Sutton.

Within a month or so Ted got a rheumatic complaint so he had to have hospital treatment so I then drove his engine, which was the 6 h.p. Garrett that I had driven quite a lot during school holidays etc., so it didn't come hard. I drove his turnout for the rest of the season.

When I wasn't threshing I would take 'Prince Henry' into a builders yard at Stalham and drive their saw benches, one was a big rack bench the other was used for cutting all off-cuts. When they got both benches fully loaded it would make Prince Henry bark, you could hear him all over Stalham Street. The engine would stand in an open shed with an extension chimney out the top I would walk away from the shed sometimes just to hear it bark, they would be going out the top there like footballs. We had to lower the chimney to get in and out of this yard as there was a store built over the entrance, it is used for workshops and all sorts of things now and the building over the entrance has been taken down so high vehicles can get in. I was the last one to take an engine into Tooley and Youngs yard. I did fifteen days sawing the last time but I don't think any more trees were bought and sawn up after that.

When I finished sawing I had to take the engine to White House Farm at Stalham which was over the railway bridge, which is no longer there having been demolished to make way for the bypass. I picked up the drum and straw pitcher and set sail for Potter Heigham. After we got through Stalham High Street I put a little coal on the fire and up the hill we came passed Bristows Mill when I saw a gentleman stop his car, which was an open topped car, they were quite popular in those days. I didn't take much notice of him until he stepped into the middle of the road and put his hand up signaling me to stop, which I did. He strutted about there for a minute or two then he said in rather a loud voice, 'I am the police superintendent from North Walsham', I didn't speak, he then said 'What's all that doing coming out up there', pointing to the funnel top.

I said, 'What do you mean!' (I had a good idea what he meant)
'I mean all that black smoke everywhere'.
So me being young and a bit cheeky said, 'That's where it should come out'.
His eyes looked as if they were about to pop out of his head. He then said, 'Have you a licence to be on that thing!' Which annoyed me a bit to call that engine a thing.
I said 'Yes, I have.'
He held out his hand for it, as it happened I had my driving licence in my pocket, but it was for riding a motor bike only. As I was only seventeen and not old enough to drive a traction engine. You couldn't drive an engine lawfully on the Highway under the age of twenty one years. I thought now I'm in for it, but he looked at my licence and handed it back without saying a word.

He then said, 'I'm afraid I shall have to make a case of this, as you know full well it is an offence to make a lot of smoke in a built up area'.
As he was asking more questions another car came along and hit the old boy's car which stood opposite us with a lady sitting in. It damaged the mudguard (they were mudguards in them days not wings) the old super went mad because the other car didn't stop. He jumped about waving his arms and sticking his fingers in his mouth and whistling like a train. He then turned to me and said,
'You saw what happened, didn't you!
I said, 'No, I weren't looking'.
'Away you go then,' and he waved me on.
I said to the fellow who was steering me, 'I've done it now'. He said, 'Don't you worry about that silly old bugger he don't know what the chimney is for'.

When I got to Sutton I stopped at Ted's house and told him what had happened, he said, I shouldn't worry too much about that, in fact I didn't ever hear any more about it.

There was a lot of Police activity at that time because the Church was claiming Tythe Money from some of the farmers in this area. They even went as far as taking furniture from the farm houses and selling it to get the money, also farm impliments were taken and sold.

This happened at the late Mr John Blaxell's farm at Potter Heigham, I was shown in the house and saw the bedroom doors broken to get the furniture out, there was a right row going on over this Tythe job.

I was moving the engine to Blaxell's farm to thresh when one of these policemen stopped me, again about smoke, he started on me about this, when I told him I had to have a fire in the engine and as a rule there is smoke come from a fire, he didn't say any more.

I finished the season with Ted, when harvest time came he was fit for work again. I enjoyed using that engine and was sorry when he came back.

The next season I was odd man out, sometimes I was feeding with Grandfather, sometimes with Ted. I did a little driving on various engines, I was now eighteen years old. I can't remember much happening out of the ordinary only plenty of hard work, mud and muck and very little money. I received eight shillings a day when it was fine and nothing when it was bad weather. I made fire shovels and pokers for household use and sold them for a few shillings. I was still doing a few cycle repairs in my little workshop in the garden.

I managed to buy a few pigs and fatted them up, when I sold them I bought a few more, and with the money I bought a Clyno car, it was a two seater with a dicky seat at the back. I bought it one Saturday morning for £11.00. I had never driven a car before but had a good idea what to do, so I drove home. Grandfather said, you must be soft to buy that thing, I didn't think so at the time but probably he was right.

Petrol was one shilling and three pence per gallon. I always bought my petrol from Mr Walsingham, who at that time had a small garage in Sutton Street next to the Chapel. He had one hand operated petrol pump and he sold R.O.P. petrol, I don't suppose you would find any in the country now, I think it was Russian.

Anyway, I bought the car in the morning and the same night away we go to Yarmouth. I think Bob Baker went with me. After the pictures it was fish and chips. We did this quite often until one Saturday night when we were coming home I found the lights started getting dimmer, so I switched off the headlights. I could see all right as the moon was bright. All went well until I reached Potter Heigham river bridge, it was now midnight and the dance hall near the bridge was turning out so four policemen were there to keep their eye on things. The traffic lights on the bridge were red so I had to stop. One of the policemen tapped on the side of the car, so I opened the door and got out. He said,
'What game are you playing'.
I said, 'What do you mean!'.
He pointed out to me that I had only one small light on the front and that was the near side.
I said, I didn't know the lights were not working. After taking my name and address he told me I couldn't drive any further so get it off the road. So we pushed it onto the straithe near the river and walked home. I fetched it early on the Sunday. About two weeks later I received a summons to appear at Rollesby Court House, which was held at the old workhouse.

I sat in the court waiting for my case to come up, another man was there on the same charge, driving with insufficient lights. He told the magistrates he knew his lights weren't working and as he hadn't far to go he thought he would try to get home. He was fined one pound five shillings. I thought I had better think of something different to him as that was a lot of money, about a week's wages. So my name was called next. They went into all the details and then asked if I had anything to say. I told them as far as I knew my lights were working all right and they must have fused as I dipped them when I met another car just up the road and with all the lights shining out of the dance hall I didn't notice the headlights weren't working. I told them I had to walk home, they all laughed. The Chairman said, 'We have decided to fine you two shillings and sixpence so be a bit more careful in the future as it is very dangerous driving a motor car with no lights'.

I paid up and got out pretty quick.

I was getting a bit of a lad by now, especially with the young ladies, having the old car was an asset, I had lots of fun in that old Clyno car.

The next Spring Billy came over and said he had got wrong with Tom King and the first chance he got he was going to move. He then wrote to Grandfather and said he had a chance to start on his own again. A farmer out that way told him that a relation of his had an engine and if he was interested he would buy it for him and he could do his threshing and pay for it as he earned it. Billy thought that a good offer, another farmer was willing to lend him the money to buy a drum and straw pitcher. He also had the promise of more work in that area. So he came over and I took him in the Clyno over to Snettisham near Hunstanton and found this engine, We found it in a farm building behind a railway crossing, it was a six horse power single crank compound Burrell, fairly old but in fairly good order. We decided it wanted a new set of tubes, but the fire box was good. Billy said he had better put some new tubes in before we attempted to drive it home which was a journey of sixty miles.

At the same time there were some threshing tackle to be sold at Mileham. We went to Mileham and inspected the machines there. A week or two later we went to this auction at Mileham, Billy bought a Garrett drum and a Maynard chaff cutter. The next move was to order a new set of tubes off G Thurlow of Stowmarket to be sent to Snettisham Station. The next Monday morning I drove to Poringland and picked up Billy and away we went to operate on his Burrell. We soon got into work and had the old tubes out. I went to the railway station and got the new tubes and transported them in the dicky seat of the Clyno. We fitted these in the boiler, got them all expanded and furreld up. We then noticed the chimney base was badly cracked so we removed it and put it in the car and went to Savages of Kings Lynn to see if they could repair it. They were most helpful, the foreman said he didn't think he could repair it but he would see if he could find up a replacement. He looked round everywhere as there were several old engines standing about there. He eventually found a base still bolted on a boiler lying upside down in the works. He got two men into work and took it off, it wasn't the right shape but we weren't worried about that. He drilled some fresh holes in so it would fit our engine. I think the whole job came to two pounds ten shillings for everything.

Back we went and fitted the base on and put the chimney back, it was a lovely job.

The next day we filled the boiler with water and put a fire in. It wasn't long before we had steam up. We gave the old engine a good run round and found everything else to be all right.

When we went back to Snettisham we took another man with us and some coal and steamed up and started the journey to Sutton via Mileham to pick up the drum and cutter. At this sale John Sandell of Worstead bought a straw pitcher and he asked Billy could we pull his pitcher home for him. I think we got on the road with the engine about three o'clock in the afternoon. Billy told me to go with the car to Mileham and oil the wheels on the drum, pitcher and cutter and make sure everything was right and tight. Away I went, I didn't hurry I knew I had plenty of time. I eventually got to Mileham, it was a lovely day so I laid on the grass and had a sleep, there wasn't a soul about. I woke up about six o'clock and did all the oiling and made sure everything was in order. I then noticed a pub just a short distance away so I thought I would have a drink and a packet of crisps. So I went in and had my refreshments and a yarn with the landlord, who I soon found out was an old engine man. I waited in Mileham until it was dark but there was no sign of the engine, I then thought I would go back and meet them. I began to wonder if anything had gone wrong, possibly a breakdown or anything could have happened, I didn't really know what to do. I started back, I followed the same road which I had come along earlier. I went back nearly to Snettisham but still not a sign. I started trying the back roads I couldn't even see a track of an engine in the road and then I came to the conclusion I was lost, I didn't know where I was. I stopped on a corner with the car head lights shining on the sign post so I could read the names of the villages on it, when I heard a voice coming from the upstair window of a cottage standing nearby, it said 'Whateryer up to!'

I said, 'I think I'm on the wrong road'.

He said, 'Where do you wanta git to!'

I said, 'Mileham.'

'You'r bloody miles away from Mileham.'

TOP *Uncle Billy threshing with the 6 h.p. Burrell which we got from Snettisham, note the chimney base which was from Savages of King's Lynn.*
BOTTOM *Uncle Ted with 'Prince Henry' at Stalham. This is the 6 h.p. Garrett which I bought and drove for several years.*

I said, 'By the way have you seen a traction engine about here tonight!'
He said, '*Yis*, I see one going along the top road about seven o'clock.'
I thought, well at least I'm still in Norfolk. It was then about eleven. He then told me which way to go, I thanked him and set sail back to Mileham. When I got back to the meadow there were still no signs of Billy or the engine, I didn't know what to do everyone in the village in bed except me. I stood there alone, not a sound, then I heard a familiar sound of a Burrell gear wheel ringing in the distance, it wasn't long before I could see their lights coming up the road. They had two gas lamps on the front so they could see all right. Billy drove onto the meadow where the drum and pitcher stood. When he got off the engine he said I expect you wondered where we had got to. I said yes, where have you been. I have been driving round trying to find you. He had stopped and asked the way and apparently someone had told them wrong so they had come a long way round. If you travelled ten or twelve miles out of your way on an engine it would put another two hours onto your journey.

Billy said, 'You can drive now, I've had enough for a little while.'
So we hooked the gear on and I pulled onto the road. I said to the chap with us, who was steering, what is the time and he said ten minutes past one. It was as dark as a grave.

Billy said he would go in front and try and find some water because the tank is nearly empty. So we started our journey homewards. I hadn't gone far when the pump stopped and I knew the tank was empty. I had a glass three quarters full so I was all right for a little while. When we got a little further I saw Billy standing beside the road, so I stopped. He said there was some water over the fence in a little pond. He didn't know if our suction pipe would reach, anyway it did so with a tank full of water I felt a bit more comfortable. The man's name who was with us was Cyril Woods, he worked for Billy then on until he retired about twenty five years later.

We travelled on slowly through the night on a strange road on a strange engine through Brisley and North Elmham to Bawdeswell after stopping for water a time or two we got to Reepham about seven o'clock. Of course it was day light then. I saw a man then opening his shop so I stopped and went into the shop and bought some cigaretts. I then asked if he had any bread and cheese but he said he wouldn't have any until his supply came in all he had were some swiss rolls so I bought some as we were getting fairly hungry and we had all the day to go. It was the first time I ever had swiss rolls for breakfast.

When we came through Cawston the tyre came off the front wheel on the chaff cutter so that meant another roadside repair job. Aylsham side of Cawston I stopped and picked up water from a place where the water is always running, I think it comes from a lake, there is a long run down to this water and then a sharpish hill away from it. When I stopped and started taking in the water I opened the firebox door, I could see the fusible plug was leaking in the top of the firebox. I put some coal on the fire and shut the door and hoped for the best. When the tank was full I gave the old engine the whip going up that hill, I suppose a bit of scale or something got in the plug because when we got on level ground I had another look in and it had stopped leaking.

When we got to Burgh Cock we stopped for a drink. Billy had been and got some coal from somewhere so when he came back with the car I told him about the plug leaking he said straight away had I been short of water, I said no, only there was a long run downhill at Cawston it might have happened then. Anyway, we arrived home about 5.30 on the Saturday night.

What a journey. When we took the plug out there was no lead left in at all. I helped him to repair the engine and drum.

That summer we painted the engine and Charlie lined her out he was a dab hand at that job. She looked like a newon. He bought a straw pitcher out Beccles way which needed a new frame so Cyril Woods, his man who was a carpenter by trade, built the new frame in Tom Skouldings barn at Toft Monks. The engine, drum and chaff cutter were ready for action.

On the evening of August 4th 1935, which was August Bank Holiday, we set out for Shotesham, that is where Billy was living, he had hired a farm house and yard. We went through Norwich about midnight, no traffic about, straight through the City, we didn't half kick up a row going up Kings Street rattling over them blocks in the road. We got to Shotesham early in the morning and Billy started threshing off the shock that day. I left and came back in the Clyno and went straight off threshing with Grandfather at High House Farm, Catfield. Charlie took the engine over after harvest as Grandfather packed up driving. I had that season feeding the drum. The following Spring I was helping Albert moving to Horning to thresh for John Tallowin. I was steering his engine, Herbert Mallett was the driver. Suddenly she dropped down one side, the back wheel laid over onto the bank and the wire rope drum dropped off. Luckily it was the near side, I was standing the opposite side steering, she steered the right hand side, this old engine was 'Alice' a big eight horse. I said to Herbert, 'What the hell was that!'
He said, 'I think the axle has broke.'
We told the man who was cycling behind to go back to Sutton and tell Albert what had happened. When he came he brought some big blocks of wood and two big bottle jacks. We found some more blocks at the nearby farm, so we jacked Alice up onto these blocks. Charlie got steam up in Totty, which was in the yard and came to Ludham and slowly pulled the old girl on the blocks off the road into a field. Charlie then hooked onto Albert's drum and pitcher and away we went to Horning and threshed there the next day. Grandfather and Albert took the broken axle out and took it home. Albert got in touch with Garretts at Leiston but they couldn't help so he telephoned Thurlows of Stowmarket who said if he could get the broken axle to their place they would make him a new one.

A few months before all this happened I had met a young lady who I thought was just right for me so my thoughts were turned to settling down but I thought I would never have enough money to keep a wife if I carried on with the job I was doing. It meant moving away into another area to get a drivers job or starting in business, but I had no money. I didn't know what to do. The thought of having my own engine was always in my mind.

When Albert went to Stowmarket I went with him we had a trailer hooked on the back of his Morris Cowley car with the axle on board, it was a heavy peice of metal or rather two peices. All went well until we went over a railway crossing, I think it was at Pulham, I said to Albert, 'You had better stop there looks as if there is something wrong with your trailer.'

When we stopped we found the draw bar was broken so we tied it up with rope and somehow got to Thurlows.

As we were going along Albert said he thought he should buy another turnout as he had more work than one set could do. I then told him what I had in mind about having a go. He said if I could get a turnout he would let me do some of his work. When we were at Thurlows I saw Mr George Thurlow and also told him about my idea. He said there was a Garrett engine and a Marshall drum in the yard if I could find some money to pay down I could have them. I forget how much he wanted for them, but I knew it was too much for me. But as I was looking round the machines which stood in their yard another man came and spoke to me. Of course we were talking engines. He then said his boss had an engine for sale right cheap. I said what do you call cheap, he said £100. He told me it stood at Thornham Magna which was on our way home. so I ask Albert if he would go round and have a look at it. So we found the engine, a 7 h.p. Ransome, we had a good look round and came to the conclusion it was in fair condition. The owners name was Mr Bull, he said he wanted £100 for it so we came away. On the way home Albert said, 'If I were you I would write to him and bid him £60 for it, I bet he will take it.'

Just after that we were threshing on a farm at Catfield and the man who was foreman there a steady sort of fellow, I always got on well with him and I was telling him about my idea, he said if I wanted to borrow some money he would help me the best he could. So we had an agreement there and then that he would let me have enough money to buy an engine. I wrote straight away to Mr Bull and bid him £60 for his engine and got a letter back accepting it. I then arranged a day for collection, Albert took me and Herbert Mallett over in his car with the trailer on the back loaded with coal. When we got there they had already got a fire going, it wasn't long before steam was up so we hooked the trailer on the back of the engine, I then gave Mr Bull his £60 and away we came. I was as pleased as a dog with two tails to think I had got my own engine. We got most of the way home that day so we left it that night and finished the journey the next day.

I went to the Norfolk Show and saw Thurlow on their stand which was always a meeting point for engine people. Mr Thurlow said they had a Garrett drum which I could have, it stood near Haverhill and if I could get to Stowmarket they would take me to see it. This I did and they agreed to send the drum to Stalham Station. Then Mr Thurlow said I suppose you will want a straw pitcher, I said yes. He then said something about money, I said I hadn't got any, he looked at me and said, I have done business with your relations for years so I suppose I will have to help you, which he did.

I took the engine to Stalham and got the drum off the truck at the station. A week or two later the straw pitcher arrived so I had my outfit. All the money I had to make a start with was £16. I got rid of the Clyno car nobody would buy it so I scrapped it as I couldn't afford to run it.

CHAPTER FIVE

IN BUSINESS WITH A THRESHING MACHINE

AUGUST 1936 was when I started, a young fellow who had been cutting bonds with us for a year or two came with me feeding the drum, his name was Roy Dixon, he knew the job all right, his relations were engine drivers. We started at Mr B Wrights of Tunstead, I did two days off the shock for a start. When we finished I asked him if he could let me have money as I was skint he gave me a cheque which I was very grateful for. I then went on helping Charlie and Ted and then back to Tunstead, I was busy all through the harvest. After harvest Albert found me a lot of work, I then started to pick up more work on my own, I think some of the farmers took pity on me as I was then only twenty years old. I managed to keep going through the winter and did several thousands of coombs. We were always paid by the score which was twenty coomb, it was twelve shillings per score so we had to thresh one hundred coomb for three pounds and pay all running costs and pay the drum feeder, it didn't leave much profit but I found it was then too much for some of the miserable old buggers. I did five barley stacks on one farm there was more thistle and rubbish than barley (there were no sprays in those days). The five days came to £14 so I didn't earn much that week. By the time I finished the season I was about as well off as when I started. I sent some money to Thurlows and paid a little off the engine so before I started the next season I was skint. I got through the summer doing odd jobs.

I have seen men following the engine along the road to find out which farm we were going to so they could try and get a days threshing. I have been stopped many a time and asked where we were going. There was very little work about for some of these people. The regular farm hands were pretty sure of their job although the pay was not all that good. There was no dole money for agricultural workers, no family allowance either. Any man with a family was hard up indeed. Some got three days a week relief work for which I think they received twelve shillings. They worked on the roads or in a gravel pit, some of the younger men did work on sugar beet lorries carting beet to Cantley Sugar Factory.

I did manage to go to Portsmouth with a cousin of mine. We hired a car and drove to the South Coast to see the Spithead review which was held off Southsea, what a wonderful sight at night all the fleet were there and a lot of foreign battle ships, they were all lit up, I enjoyed it. We slept on the beach and came home the next day, it was to celebrate the Coronation of King George VI.

Harvest time came round and I was threshing again. It was not a very good season as the corn didn't yield very well so I couldn't earn much money. In fact I was in a muddle from start to finish. I remember giving T. W. Page, a welding engineer from Sprowston a cheque for a welding job he did. It was for £3.8s.od, the Bank Manager stopped the cheque because I hadn't enough in my account to cover it. Some of the small farmers and even one or two of the bigger ones were about as hard up as I was. These were very hard times and looking back I sometimes wonder how I survived.

During the summer of 1938 I was at Ludham one evening visiting my young lady. She worked at Ludham Hall for the late Mr W Wright who farmed a lot of land. He owned three farms at Ludham, also farms at Ingham, Stalham and Catfield. Charlie was doing the threshing on some of the farms but they did their own at Ludham. They made such a mess that in the finish Mr Wright asked me if I could do his threshing on the Ludham farms. I of course, was only too pleased to oblige. I did his threshing for years and when Charlie packed up I did the lot which was seven farms. That harvest was a good one and I did three thousand coomb of barley straight from the field before starting on the stacks. Come Michaelmas that year William Sloper who was team-man at Ludham Hall, and later became my father-in-law , decided to move to another job at Southwood near Freethorpe. That left my future wife at Ludham, so we decided to get married, but I had to find somewhere to live. There was an empty house on Stalham Green with two thirds of an acre of land and a good size shed which Billy had before things went wrong for him. It was owned by Mr John Rudd Turner, who farmed at Happisburgh. So the next Saturday evening I went to see Mr Turner. I told him I wanted to hire the house at Stalham. I had heard before I saw him that the house was let and another person told me it was sold, so I didn't know what to expect. Anyway he did seem interested, he then said he would let me know. When I left him I didn't know what to think, I had given him my address to write to. When I came home from work about four days later Grandmother said a letter had come for me that morning. When I opened it I saw it was from Mr Turner to say I could have the house and land and that he would send me the key on October 11th, which was the next week. The rent was £26 a year to be paid quarterly, I didn't say anything to Grandmother at the time but she soon found out and didn't half carry on. You will never afford that rent she said, I said I don't suppose I will ask you for the money if I can't. I think she was annoyed because I hadn't told her anything about it. Anyway, my future wife and her mother soon prepared the house. We went to Norwich and bought some furniture, I told the people whom we bought it from that I couldn't pay for it right away they said they would give me credit until I could find the money, which I did six months later.

On 16th November 1938 we were married at Freethorpe Methodist Chapel. We have recently celebrated our Golden Wedding Anniversary. When we first lived at Stalham we had no electricity, all the drinking water had to be pumped, soft water for washing was got from tubs which held the water from the roof. We had a coal fired oven in the living room-cum-kitchen, the copper was in the wash house near the house. We hadn't been there many weeks when we had electricity installed but all we had was three lights, we couldn't afford an electric kettle.

The first week of our married life I had yellow jaundice, I recovered after about a week and started work, we couldn't afford a honeymoon. I just got going when I had some trouble with my Ransome engine, I called and saw Ted and asked him if I could use his Garrett which was in the yard as he was using the Burrell, which he bought. He said he would sell it to me, so I

My wife and myself just before we were married This was taken in 1938.

agreed a price and said I would pay him at the end of the season. I think I was two years paying him. I then sold the Ransome after having some welding done on the firebox.

The following year our first son was born. In the September War was declared. Mr Turner, my Landlord, asked me if I could do his threshing, the people who had been doing it sold out so I got quite a lot of work in Happisburgh I now had a big run of work, it took all my time to keep up with it all. I had to sign on for National Service. I think it was about 1941 I had a letter saying as I was employed in agriculture my call up would be deferred but I would have to do a part-time service, so I joined the National Fire Service and was a fireman until the war was over. I did some driving, I used to man one of the pumps. We attended several plane crashes we also were on duty in Norwich when the City was bombed, this happened in between seasons so it didn't stop me from threshing.

In 1942 Ted told me he was packing up, I think he got the wind up when there were some incendiary bombs dropped near him one morning when he was getting up steam. He said Jerry saw the fire shining from the ash pan of his engine, so I said would he sell me his outfit, but he said no because he wanted to sell it away. I believe he thought I wouldn't pay him so he sold the whole outfit to a farmer and contractor in mid-Norfolk and he was two years getting his money, so he would have done no worse if he had sold it to me.

He got himself a job at T. W. Pages, he stopped and ask me if I wanted a few weeks work as they were very busy. So I thought why not. There was a few weeks before harvest, my outfit was ready so I had about four weeks helping them, I quite enjoyed myself there and the money came in handy. I repaired and fitted several small boilers in farm buildings for sterilising food for pigs, farmers collected all the waste from military canteens and cooked it. I got the job of collecting a Robey Roll which stood in a yard near a pub in Barrack Street in Norwich, a bomb had dropped nearby and blew the chimney off. The lagen was full of holes one or two other bits were broken, I had a young lad with me so we filled the boiler with water to test for leaks, there were none so I bolted the chimney back on, the blast had broken the bolts. I lit a fire and hoped for the best, it soon had steam up. A casting was broken which held the gear lever so I found a bit of wire and soon repaired that. It poured with rain as I was climbing the hill in Silver Road, when I was nearing the top the wheels started spinning. I had a job to get to the top but after backing once or twice I made it.

Mr Page sent Ted and myself to Suffield to get a Fowell engine, when we found it the back axle was bent and the gearing were lying about everywhere, it looked like a scrap engine. Ted he started mobbing about coming after a heap of scrap but after he cooled down we loaded the axle onto the truck we had and took it to Soames of Marsham. I saw Babs Cushion who was a first class engineer, he said at first that he couldn't do anything with it. After a little encouragement he said all right come on lets have a go. So we humped it onto the forge and heated it up then laid it on some blocks and give it a few clouts with a bout hammer. When it had cooled off we heaved it onto his big lathe, he gave it a twiri then he said, there you are what about that and it was just about true. By the time we got back to Suffield it was time to go home. Next day we started to put the old engine back into one piece and finished her off the following morning. We filled up with water and lit a fire in her. She soon started to get on the boil it was just dinner time so I sat down against one of the front wheels Ted he said, 'I arn't sitting near her the old bugger might blow up.'

I laughed and told him not to talk so bloody soft.

The next morning we left home early and steamed up and set sail for Norwich. Ted wouldn't get on the engine, he said 'I'll drive the motor behind.' I think he knew what he was on because when I got onto the main road I had a rough ride as someone had put five new strakes on one wheel and everytime they come round and hit the road I got a nasty jolt.

Page sold it to Webb of Woodton who used it for threshing one or two seasons then if finished up sterilising soil at some glass houses. I then finished at Pages and did a bit more work at home.

By now Ted had sold his outfit and it had gone, we took it as far as Sprowston Blue Boar and met Mr Law and his men who took it to Hockering. So I thought I would have to do something about the customers which he had, so I went round all of them and told them I was getting another turnout so I could carry on with their threshing and everbody said yes. The biggest customer was surprised to think Ted had sold out as he hadn't told any of them. He said what was I doing for money to buy this other machine with. I said I shall have to find some from somewhere, he said he would stand security for me at the Bank. I didn't tell any of my relations about the arrangement I had made at the Bank.

Arthur Haylett, who was a threshing contractor at Wroxham, was retiring and selling his machinery so on the 12th of July 1942 I went to his auction, my cousin Jack went with me. I bought a Burrell single crank compound engine with a Ransome drum and straw pitcher. The engine was fairly old, built 1900 No: 2335. Roy Dixon who had been my drum feeder for six years was getting handy so he drove the Garrett turnout and I took the Burrell engine.

After I had got all this organised Charlie went and sold his drum and pitcher without telling me but he still had the engine and chaffcutter. I went and saw him and bought the cutter which was a very good one. The engine which was Grandfather's old engine was still in the yard. Gladden and Co., came along and bought it because Jack, my cousin, who drove their engine was just making a start that season when he had a calamity on the road. The pin came out of the crosshead, it smashed the trunk and doubled the piston rod up, the connecting rod was bent like a walking stick, I never saw such a mess. I told him it was his fault, he put a new pin in the crosshead and I told him he hadn't done the nuts up properly, he said he had, but I had my doubts. Anyway, he used the Garrett that season. Gladdens never did know the full story about that job.

The next summer they ask me if I could get the Marshall going again. They had been in touch with Marshalls, all they could send them was a new piston rod I heard on the grape vine that there was a Marshall engine standing at Marsham which was being scrapped so I bought the trunk and crosshead the only snag it was a 7 h.p. engine so after a bit of altering and scheming I got the old girl going again. Jack was pleased, he liked his engine the best, he was always mobbing about the Garrett.

I then bought the Garrett better known as Totty No: 29009, and used it instead of the Burrell. When I got her I could see what Jack was swearing about. In 1943 we built a shed big enough to put a drum and straw pitcher in, we found this very handy.

That same summer Norman Beck, who farmed Brumstead Hall, bought a new Ransome drum and I built him a straw pitcher. Some of the larger farmers started doing that when they got tractors on the job. I had already built one straw pitcher from a large plank of wood which washed up on the beach at Eccles, it was pine. A man I knew pulled it over the hills with horses, I bought it off him, it was about thirty feet long, two feet wide and a foot thick, I just about built two straw pitchers from that one piece of wood. George Plummer, who had a saw yard at Stalham with a big rack bench cut it up for me.

The next harvest I had so much work I couldn't keep up so I went to a sale at Ormesby when George Barrett sold out and bought a Marshall drum and pitcher so I then had three sets. I got another fellow driving the Burrell, I took the Garrett and Marshall drum onto the marshes at Ludham near St Benets Abbey and threshed all the wheat and oats that was grown there that year, I often think when I hear all the squit that's made about ploughing these marshes up if people concerned only knew what they were talking about they would know it does good to plough a marsh up now and again. The ones that were cropped during the War are the best marshes on that level.

A few years ago we had some men and machines working on those marshes cleaning the dykes out and levelling some spoil which had been there for years when all of a sudden they were surrounded by some of these people shouting something about spoiling the country side. One of our drivers got a bit stroppy and grabbed one of these fellows and told him if he didn't bugger off he would put him in the dyke. It worked because they didn't bother them any more, and we got a free advert on television.

As I said, the Garrett engine I bought from Gladden & Co wasn't behaving too well but I got it through the season. I could see why Jack was swearing about it. Charlie had it for six years and the only repairs to be done was straking the back wheels. Anyway, I got to work on it and like a fool spent a lot of money repairing it. I fitted a new set of boiler tubes bored the cylinder, fitted a new piston, new slide valves, trued the valve face, all new pins in the link motion and bushed all the glands, she ran like a new one. I painted and lined her out she was very smart and then a few years later she was scrapped. That was one big mistake.

Just before harvest Albert came to me and said he had one of his men hand in his notice to leave so he offered me the outfit and all the work that went with it and said I could have his driver so being young and silly I took it on. I was still driving one set myself and it was keeping me busy then things started to go wrong. Roy Dixon was threshing for Mr Sands at Stalham when the drum came to a sudden stop they said there was a loud bang. It was then that a lot of live ammunition was found in the sheaves of wheat, I should think some of these things exploded inside the drum, it smashed it up completely so it was out of action for the rest of the season, it had to be examined by an inspector from the Ministry of defence, also the insurance company. I was paid compensation, but after I paid for the hire of a drum from the war Agricultural Department and repaired my drum I was still out of pocket. I had another drum brake one of the driving springs on the riddle crank. It flung round and bent the crank so this was another expense and loss of time.

During the War all threshing contractors or any farmer who did the job himself had to send in grain return forms every week for all the grain we done. They were more interested in the wheat, all had to be worked out into Tons and Cwts. One day a gentleman called on me and said he wanted to see my books about some wheat one of my drivers had done on a farm. This farmer had kept several coomb of wheat to feed his poultry with. This was against the law. Wheat at that time was very short as some of the ships bringing wheat from abroad had been sunk by enemy action. This farmer had a stack the top of which was oats the rest of the stack was wheat. He gave my driver a drink to book less wheat and more oats. The trouble started when he sacked his poultry man who in turn notified the Ministry. The returns I sent in didn't match the farmers returns. I gave him my books but he couldn't make it out at all. I couldn't help because I didn't know. The next day two more men came to see my books and they were very important people, one I happened to know. At one time he had a smallholding at Stalham but went bankrupt. He then got the job of coming round and telling other people how a business should be run. I said to them I wasted a half day yesterday over this job with some fellow. One of them said this other man was a detective so I had better watch what I was doing or I would be getting mighty wrong. I said I hadn't done anything wrong, it looked to me as if them lot were trying to make me carry the can for somebody else and they wanted to find out a bit more about it before they put the blame on me. I then called to see the farmer involved. He said there was nothing to worry about and that everything was all right. I said, I didn't know so much about that and that I had three fellows to see me about it. He said he thought they were trying to frighten me, but I said I wasn't too happy about it. Anyway, it got hushed up somehow. I received a nasty letter telling me I didn't keep my accounts properly.

It was sometime after that I heard the truth about it. The farmer heard somehow that they were coming to try and find this wheat, he sent it all into the Merchants, it was then put out of reach. Anyhow, I didn't hear any more about it.

When those fellows came to see me abut this wheat job I thought at first they were from the Council because when we built the shed to put a drum in I didn't have any planning permission. We painted the wood with some dull paint so it didn't look new in case somebody did come and have a look. I didn't ever see anyone, anyway it isn't much good coming now because the shed is long gone.

The next summer Jack who drove Gladden's engine said he was going to work full-time on his smallholding, he always did keep pigs and poultry. That meant he would be finishing with threshing and he had been talking to his employers and rather than take on a new driver would I be interested in buying their turnout and carry on doing all their customers' work. It was their 8 h.p. Marshall with a Garrett drum and straw pitcher and an Innes Six Knife Chaff Cutter with all spares and hand tools, it was a big temptation. My wife didn't want me to have anything to do with it, but I did. I had to borrow the money to pay for it. That was another big mistake, I was getting too big, I found I couldn't earn money quick enough to meet my outgoings. I carried on like this for two seasons and I was still in a muddle, I didn't tell my wife too much about things as she had her hands full as we had by then got seven children. I was getting a bit of aggro from some of the men I had working for me, one fellow who was a drum feeder knew all the answers he was also a red hot Union man, he educated all the others.

One morning we were in the yard getting ready for harvest some were working the others were hiding up. I called them all together and told them I had made up my mind to sell out. I gave them all notice to leave, I called the best fellows to one side and asked them if they would keep with me after the sale as I had made up my mind to keep two sets and keep the best customers. I had an auction and retained two outfits but I found I had to buy another one as the customers kept coming. I was then running three sets, I was still driving one myself, I had cleared my debts so I was working more comfortable but still things didn't seem to go right. The next harvest was terrible, it rained nearly every day and in November my wife fell down stairs and cut her leg so bad the doctor had to put sixteen stitches in, things didn't go well at all.

In January it started to snow and it did really come down. It filled all the roads so nothing

Grandfather when he was young on the front of the Portable Engine, also his father and brothers Tom and Albert taken at Acle about 1875.

TOP *Albert on his 7 h.p. Marshall threshing at Sutton. This engine is restored and still in Norfolk.*
BOTTOM *Cousin Jack threshing with the 8 h.p. Marshall and Garrett Drum at Brumstead Hall for Mr Norman Beck in the 1930's.*

could move we would walk to the engines and keep a fire going so they didn't freeze up but there was no money coming in, this went on for weeks. We managed to do a few days now and again. Snow was with us until April. I hired a bulldozer from H. P. E. Neave of Catfield to help my engines along the road to get from one farm to another, of course, this was all extra expence. I noticed not many of the customers offered to help, we did eventually finish the season.

I bought a big saw bench and when we couldn't thresh I kept the men busy sawing up trees I sold the planks of wood to farmers and builders and all the offcuts I cut into firewood logs which I sold to householders.

When we were working on threshing machines for a livelyhood I have known a lot of people who would run the other way if they thought they were needed to help. There was too much muck for them, now they pay to see them working, how things have changed.

The next harvest I bought a tractor, it was an International W. 30. Cousin Tom made a winch and fitted on, the fellows who were driving my other two engines laughed and thought I was silly. They said it would never get the drum about when it was really bad weather but I proved them wrong. It would drive the drum and wire baler just as good as the steam engine did, much to my surprise.

One day I met Harry Neave of Catfield he was the man who was the owner of the bulldozers, that side of the business was known as Catfield Grain Company Limited. He had fourteen farms ran as Catfield Farms also the works at Catfield where he started it all at Bleak House Farm. Poultry houses and all sorts of buildings were made there during the war they were building landing craft for the Army, also incubators for the chicken industry and fridges of all sizes were made there. He really was in big business. At one time he employed a thousand people.

The late Mr Sidney Grapes, who wrote the Boy John letters in the Eastern Daily Press, was riding passed Neaves works one day with another man when he was asked how many people worked there, Sidney, who was a comedian said 'About half on em'.

Anyway, I met Mr Neave and he said, 'Jimmy, I want you to come and work for me'.

After a bit of thought I said that if he bought my old threshing tackle, steam engines and all we would have a deal, which we did.

I was only too pleased to see the back of them, I was sick of the sight of them when he bought them I thought thank God for that. I was put in charge of the threshing side plus a few other things. He also employed all my men. We all knew that the days for threshing with the steam engine were numbered. I signed to say I wouldn't start threshing in this area inside five years but he need not have worried because by the next February he passed away before reaching the age of fifty.

After I had been with the Grain Company a few months my Uncle at Shotesham gave up his threshing job as he had built up another business building trailers and straw pitchers and general engineering. I knew there was plenty of work round there so I bought a Marshall tractor, there was a Garrett drum standing in his yard which belonged to a dealer, I bought it and a straw pitcher. Billy and Tom got the customers organised. Ted by now was more or less free so I introduced him to the head man at Catfield and handed in my notice. They were not very pleased, I told them that the job weren't for me, I couldn't stick other people looking over my shoulder all the time.

I worked the next season in the Shotesham area but kept living at Stalham, I nearly bought a house in that area at one time but as things turned out I am glad I didn't. I travelled everyday except for about six weeks when I lodged at Saxlingham. Petrol was still on coupons at that time and I had used my coupons so I had to stop there until I was allocated some more.

After Mr Neave's death everything was sold. All the farms and machinery the works were closed I went to the sale when the threshing tackle were sold and bought a few things. I had seen some of my old customers and they all said if I came back and started again in that area I could have their work. I bought a modern Ransome drum on pneumatic tyres and a new Marshall tractor so I then had two modern outfits and plenty of work. I had that winter bought a new wire baler. Tom got himself fixed up with a new Marshall drum and pitcher and carried on with the customers which I had the previous year so everyone was happy. I drove one turnout Roy Dixon drove the other one, we had plenty of work. We were busy throughout the year when the threshing season finished we had plenty of baling, it was wire baling in those days. After that we did use quite a lot of thick baler twine, there were very few pick up balers about. I did a bit of buying and selling of hay and straw, I had a market for it in the Newmarket area. By then I had a decent car and also a van. I still have the two Marshall tractors.

ABOVE *Threshing peas with Garrett 6 h.p. No. 27556 'Prince Henry'. This was at Hall Farm, Stalham. Mr D. King in the foreground.*

BELOW *The Burrell Compound Threee Speed Engine which Tom and myself brought from Palgrave.*

CHAPTER SIX

MORE TRACTION ENGINE STORIES

One summer I went to a sale of threshing machines at Otley in Suffolk, Albert rode with me. When we got to the sale we met Billy who was there with a dealer friend of his. Albert said a farmer he knew wanted to buy a drum to do his own threshing he thought it would be cheaper, several tried that but when they found what it really involved it didn't work out so cheap after all. So he bought a Garrett drum for this farmer, he said he would earn himself a few pound. The machinery dealer also bought a Garrett drum, Billy bought a Garrett tractor. When the sale was over Billy asked me if I would help him to get these things to Shotesham, so we hooked the two drums together and coupled up to the engine. We hooked my car on the back Albert steered the car, Billy then went off to get my cousin Tom also some coal. Then I set sail driving and steering this little 4 h.p. engine with two drums hanging on behind. I got plenty of steam on and a glass full of water, I was getting along nicely, I had never had any thing to do with a Garrett tractor before I'd always had a big engine, anyway, I soon got used to it. I was heading for Debenham when I approached this steep down hill which I didn't know was there until I was on it I couldn't stop and change gear it was too late so I had to hold that lot the best I could. The weight I had on behind was giving me a good old push I should think we were going down that hill about fifteen miles an hour, I had a job to keep her in the road. I couldn't reach the brake I had the reversing lever over in reverse but she kept rolling, I eventually got control and breathed a sigh of relief. There was not so many cars about in those days otherwise there might have been a calamity. After turning the corner at the bottom of this hill I stopped. Albert came up to the engine and said, 'You were getting a move on down that hill weren't you!'
I said, 'Yes.'

It was too quick for my liking I couldn't hold her, if I had three hands I would have been all right. I got between Debenham and Eye before Billy got back with Tom. I had a steersman then. We stopped and filled up with water at Eye I then heard the church clock strike twelve midnight our lights weren't very good so Tom walked in front going through Eye with a bicycle lamp I then followed him. When we got clear of Eye I said to Tom, you can drive now I'll steer, we arrived at Shotesham as it was getting day light.

On another occasion Tom said that Ronald Clark had asked him if he could fetch an engine from Frank Stevens of Palgrave near Diss. He asked me if I would go with him. So on a Saturday morning in February away we go after picking up Mr Clark and another gentleman who came for a ride. We made our way to Palgrave in Tom's old Citreon car, I think we had some bags of coal tied on the back with two cans of oil, we filled up with water and got up steam. Frank Stevens said to Tom and me he was glad to see us boys there with Mr Clark as he was worried when he said he was coming to get the engine as he couldn't imagine him driving her to Norwich. It was a three speed double crank compound engine on springs, a lovely machine, it is still around somewhere, I don't know where.

It was one o'clock when we came through Diss and we were at Shotesham before four o'clock. She could really get a move on, the injectors worked perfectly, and everything went well for the whole trip.

Mr Hudson Barber was a farmer who lived at Street Farm, Catfield, he also farmed White House Farm and Heath Farm, and also Lound Farm, Sea Palling. He had a threshing turnout, Arthur Riseborough, better known as Jack, he drove it for years, it was built by Paxmans of Colchester it was new in 1911. It was bought from the Royal Show that year. This Paxman engine was a well built machine but it never seemed to have a lot of go and it never did seem to govern too well on the drum. When Mr Barber died his farms and other business was ran by executors, one was Mr S Mowle of Happisburgh.

One Sunday afternoon he came and asked me if I could go to Eccles and pull Jack out. He had dropped in on the Saturday and he was still there trying to get the engine out, I said it was too late that day by the time I had gone to my engine and got up steam it would be dark. Anyway, I went to Eccles and see Jack he was well and truly stuck. Daisy, that was the name of his engine, was in right up to the hubs of the back wheels. They had dug down and got some wood under the wheels but she wouldn't lift herself out so I arranged with him to get my man Roy, who was threshing the next day at Sutton, to go and give him a pull as soon as he had finished. I then went and told Roy what to do. Jack was uncle to Roy.

So the next day after he finished his stack he went over and pulled Jack out. When I had finished I went and saw Roy, who was then back with his engine ready for the next day, I said 'What have you got Daisy out!'

Roy said, 'Ya, she come out there behind me like a broken winded Dickey'

I thought that just about summed it all up.

When the executors finally decided to sell out all the farms were sold and then the threshing set. Steam was just about on its last legs, the engine was sold for £21.00.

Wesley Key bought the engine, Uncle Albert bought the drum. Wesley asked me if I would stand the engine in my yard until he decided what to do with it. I did use it threshing for a few days just to see what she really was like. I did get it to govern herself fairly but there was always a mist coming from her chimney. She was a wet steamer, I didn't like it at all, so I stood her back in the yard.

Jack by then was working with us as odd hand sacking corn. I then got a message from Wesley asking could I get the engine to Worstead as some farmer there wanted to pull some trees down. So I said to Jack would he take the old engine to Worstead, he was pleased with the job. So one morning away he go on his own, I told him I would pick him up later on. As soon as I was clear I went to get Jack home. When I got about two miles away I saw a chimney lying on the verge, I knew where it came from, it was a heavy cast iron chimney, Burrell type. When I was nearly in Worstead I could see Jack going along the road without a funnel on. I have never seen anything so funny, poor old Jack was nearly in tears. He had then passed one of

This is the Garrett Tractor I brought from Otley in Suffolk with two drums behind which nearly got away with me coming down a steep hill.

Aldridge's turnouts threshing, them fellows were laughing, Jack said, 'They are all teerkin the p**s at me.'

Poor old Jack died in hospital the following summer, I saw him just before he went in and he said he was going to have his tubes cleaned.

I went to a sale with Ted and Roy Dixon at Attleburgh, it was for a Mr Beales who had about six turnouts, it was 1937. I remember there was a five foot Burrell Drum also some Holmes Drums. Some of the engines were very old but I remember two more modern Burrells. Ted bought an old engine and sold it to Jack Jarvis of Honing near North Walsham to drive his sawbench. He had a Wallace tractor but the firebox was bad so he replaced it with the Burrell. I bought a Maynard Chaffcutter at the sale.

After the sale we hooked the cutter on and made tracks for home. By the time we got to Hethersett it was dark so we pulled into a farmyard and came home by car. I had an old Morris Cowley car. On the way home the big ends began to knock I kept heading homewards, I don't think there was any metal left in them bearings by the time we got home.

The next morning we went in Ted's car and got the engine, I drove it home. When we arrived in Norwich we couldn't come through the city so we turned off Newmarket Road into Queens Road to Bracondale. As we were going towards Bracondale and then Riverside I noticed the suction pipe was dragging on the road so I stopped and Roy got down and hooked it up. While we were stopped I saw a man walking passed with two greyhounds on a lead. When I started moving the old engine barked out and it didn't half echo in those houses. Well

The 8 h.p. Burrell which Ted drove to Burrell's to have a new half barrell and a new cylinder fitted. It was built in 1891. Still in Norfolk it is now called the Big A.

those dogs took off, the last time I saw them they were going up the road about thirty miles an hour with their owner in hot pursuit. I don't know if he ever did catch them.

We were threshing on a farm when everything was frozen solid everytime I sucked some water in, I had to take the suction pipe off quick and hang in on the boiler to stop it freezing up. The water cart was more than half full of ice so by the time they got the tank up to the engine there weren't a lot of water left in. The farmer, who was an old man, said we were using a lot of water that day. I tried to explain the trouble but he didn't seem to believe me. Anyway, I went on the drum to give Roy a spell, when he got down he thought he would have a go at getting some of this ice out of the tank so he took the crowbar and set about it, the next thing was he put the bar through the bottom, so that messed the thing up altogether. The boss man weren't very pleased, but he did have another tank so we could keep going.

This same farmer hadn't a lot of time for us young fellows he wouldn't leave us far, he wouldn't allow any smoking. I would get down in the tender so he couldn't see me and have a crafty smoke. The fellow who was sacking corn said to me he thought the old man was a dam nuisance, he was always in his way. I said to him pull the sack barrow over his foot with a coomb on. The next thing I saw was William hopping out of the field on his dock spade, which he always used for a walking stick. We didn't see anymore of him that day.

This farmer provided us with beer, we were there one day when it was very hot and the stack was cut about by rats and mice, it was a really mucky job. The men were thirsty they drunk nine gallons that day. He would also bring beer when it was very cold but nobody wanted it so I used to pour it into the tank on the engine. She liked it. Some would give us a jug of tea, but not many.

When we had finished on that farm I had to move about three quarters of a mile to the next job and it was all up hill. The road was covered deep in snow and it was still freezing like a knife it took us from half past three until nine o'clock that night before I got set against the stack. It was then a seven mile journey home. I got home about half past ten. Roy had a further three miles to go I don't think these traction engine enthusiasts would think much of that. It didn't stop there, we had to be back again early the next morning in those sort of road conditions we had to walk half way there.

I was threshing for a farmer at How Hill, Ludham his name was Harry Drake. I was pulling into a field one night it was getting dark, I had just got the engine off the road with the drum and pitcher still in the road when down go Charlie Burrell right on the edge of a muck heap, it was right in all this juice and it didn't smell too healthy either. I told Ted George, who was my drum feeder, to pull the rope out at the front so we put it round the front and back onto a tree which stood in a plantation on our left hand side. When I started to pull the old engine laid right over. Poor old Mr Drake said, 'You will turn her over Jimmy.'
I said, 'She w'unt go over.'
I kept pulling and out she came, it was by now dark, I am sure us old engine men developed cats eyes so we could see in the dark. I do sometimes take a ride round those narrow roads to How Hill some parts have big dykes each side and I wonder how on earth we got a threshing turnout round there in the dark, sometimes we had the chaffcutter on the back too. I have been told that you can still see a mark on the tree I fixed my wire rope on.

At Hickling near the Broad there is a stretch of land which is called the Stubb, it have a narrow lane with farms each side running down to the marshes. It was very wet land years ago before drainage was done. I have had some fun and games down there.

I moved to Willow Farm from Ludham. As we stopped and took in water from the Broad it started raining so things were getting pretty wet by the time we got to the stacks. I got the engine off the road and roped the drum and pitcher in, by this time it was nine o'clock and we were wet through and the engine was in nearly up to the hubs of the back wheels. The next morning we managed to get the engine out and got the drum in between the stacks we had a hell of a job I lost my temper a time or two and started swearing about putting stacks in such a place, it was dinner time before we got set. There was a man helping us to lift the railway sleepers about which we put under the wheels, he was a bit religious so everytime I come out with a mouthful he would say 'Pray short Jimmy'.

One of my drivers was coming round the edge of the broad over what is known as Hill Common, with the chaffcutter on the back of the turnout and the fellow steering didn't keep up far enough so the cutter left the road and finished upside down in the broad that caused some nasty words when I saw it but that didn't help to get it out.

I was chaffcutting on a farm one Saturday morning it was about a week before Christmas when the farmer came and paid the odd men who were helping he gave me our board money and then he said would I be offended if he gave me £1.00 for my children, I said I certainly would not be offended, I then thanked him very much. I thought at first he meant £1.00 each.

One farmer came to me one day moaning about the men, he said they weren't working hard enough. It was because the stack we were threshing which he thought was going through before dinner was taking all day. It was a stack of peas they had to pitch them all onto the drum head wind and they were covered in muck. Anyone who had had anything to do with threshing peas know it isn't a very nice job. When he had finsihed moaning I told him he could see it was a dirty old job and that them fellows were only human beings the same as he was. He looked at me as if he had never realised that before and said he supposed they were. He stood behind the engine and howled big crocodile tears. I then told him he wanted to think himself lucky that anybody came after him at all, some of them used to make me very angry sometimes.

When a new water main was laid in some of the villages around Stalham a firm from Wymondham did the job. They bought a steam roller to roll the trenches. The agent called and asked me if I could get this engine going as it hadn't been used for some time, it was brought to my place on a low loader. The boiler inspector came and passed the boiler okay. I then steamed it and supplied them with a driver for the summer, it did at one time belong to Monument and Ray, the name plate was bolted to the side. It was a Burrell single crank compound engine with four shaft gearing, which was very unusual as nearly all Burrells were three shaft I think these contractors bought this machine for £15.00.

Another man I threshed for at Hickling had some funny sayings. I was there one morning when I noticed one of the tractor tyres were flat, he said, 'What dyer reckon is a matter with it!' I said, 'It look as if it is short of wind Joe.'

I went into one of his fields one night in the dark and knocked the gate post over. After we had finished and moved away one of his men said we had better put that post up again what Jimmy knocked over. Joe said, 'You had better leave it because he have to go in there agin and will only knock the bugger down agin.'

I was working with my man Roy threshing at Hempstead. We worked together at the end of the season, I was bond cutting when another farmer from Stalham came and said he had a horse stuck in a drain on a marsh could I take a tractor with a winch on and pull it out. So I had a word with the man we were working for and he said he would help Roy while I was gone. I then went home and started my other tractor and away I go. When I arrived I could see the poor old horse was well and truly stuck only his head could be seen. They had fixed a rope around his neck, Mr Farmer and his men hooked my rope on, he said away you go. When I started to pull the old horse's neck stretched out straight I stopped pulling. The farmer started to shout go on pull, I said I'm not pulling him like that, I'll pull his head off. So we dug down around his backside and put the rope round him when I pulled I made sure the horse was not hurt I dragged him out he couldn't stand at first. When he got the use of his legs back he went round that marsh like a race horse. The farmer used to help to Grade bullocks at Stalham Sale so he said, thank Jack for letting you come away and I will make it up to him when he send some bullocks up. So I told Jack what he said. When I saw him sometime after that I said to him how did he get on with his cattle, he swore and said they had given him a low grade and he would know what to do next time he helped him out.

I went into a field at Potter Heigham to thresh a wheat stack for Mr Playford who was called

Ruff, he also owned the Post Office and was also the village postman. At that time some of the farmers were having their land gyrotilled, it was a craze for a little while, it didn't last long. It was a track laying machine with two big revolving sets of tines on the back it stirred the land to a depth of about two feet deep. Well, Ruff had this field done, before I got the drum up against the stack the engine was in nearly up to the hubs. We hadn't any wood near to put under the wheels so I packed up and left her. Ted was threshing about a mile away so he came the next morning and ran his rope through the hedge and pulled me out. We then did the stack, that was another little episode over.

I was threshing on another farm when the Boss said he wanted to show me something in the barn as he had found a little corn in some straw I had threshed the previous time I was there. He was moaning about this with his broken arm stuck out on a board. He had been thrown out of his cart when his horse went down. When we came out he tripped over the 'troshall' (Threshold), he couldn't save himself because of his arm so he went down nose first into about a foot deep of pigs muck. He looked a pretty sight when I helped him up as he always had about four days growth on his chin, I dare not let him see me laughing.

I was threshing on a farm at Hickling and the stack was wet and the sheaves were grown together so the men threw all this wet stuff onto the ground. When we finished the stack the farmer said to me are you putting that lot through, meaning all the wet stuff. I said, no we couldn't do anything with that. He got a bit angry and said he bet if that was mine I would put it through I said if it were mine it wouldn't be in that state anyway. As he was walking away he said, I know you, y'are a clever sort of a bugger.

Threshing at Hall Farm, Stalham. Charlie is the driver.

At a rally with Prince Charles.

CHAPTER SEVEN

LOCAL CHARACTERS

SUTTON AND the surrounding villages had their share of old characters or at least they seemed to be to us younger people. Some of them seemed to get the job of chaff sacking with a threshing drum. There was Goff Wiley, he didn't do any work for years he hurt his arm lifting something and he played on that until all his club money and other hand-outs ran out. He eventually came with us threshing, I went to his house to see him when they opened the door I couldn't hardly see Goff, the stove was smoking he sat near it smoking his pipe. It was like a thick fog. He spent quite a bit of time in the Catherine Wheel, the local pub.

When he was working with Albert he helped him to move his turnout but he didn't get paid, I think he was told it was all part of his day's work but Goff didn't think so. Albert had a big garden and he used to grow lettuces and various things and his wife would sell them at the door. So she put put a board on the gate advertising the lettuces. When a customer came along she went down the garden to cut some and found they were gone. Sometime after that he was chaff sacking with me, when we were having our dinner Roy, my drum feeder was pulling Goff's leg about these lettuces and said he believed Goff took them. He said, well he can't expect me to help him to move for nothing.

Goff's wife was a hard working little woman, she was only about four feet six inches high. She went into the Catherine Wheel to get a glass of stout, it was the first day for a new landlord. He looked over the counter and said 'I am not allowed to serve anyone under the age of eighteen.' Hannah said, 'I am over sixty.'

When the Americans were about here during the War Hannah went to Stalham and called in at the Maids Head. This little woman amused these Yanks, they treated her to several drinks until Hannah couldn't walk. She always pushed a pram where ever she went so they put her in the pram and pushed her down Stalham Street and then left her to sleep it off behind a hedge. She never had any children of her own but she brought up several children who came from an orphanage.

Another one who did the chaff job for years lived at Catfield he walked everywhere. He lived on his own and spent most of his money in the pub, then a widow woman came along and married him, her name was Rosie, her first husband was a chimney sweep. She wasn't all that particular but she did make sure the old man had some food. His name was George Thompson, he was always called Jiver.

He was threshing at Horning when he saw a big old doe hare hanging on the gate post so he said to Mr Tallowin, the farmer, 'Can I have har.'
He said, 'Yes, of course you can.'

Me with the Marshall Model M Tractor.

So home he went that night with this great big hare hanging on his back its ears were nearly touching the road. The next day one of the men there said, 'I suppose you will have hare for tea tonight Jiver!'
He said, 'No, we hed har interus about fower o'clock as mornin.'

One morning it was a bit wet so Albert stopped at Jiver's to see if he wanted a lift but the old man was gone. Albert knocked on the door, Rosie thinking it was Jiver home again said come in, but he knocked the second time so she shouted, 'Come in you silly old bugger don't stand there in the rain.'
So he opened the door only to find Rosie standing there in her bloomers, he shut the door right quick.

Jiver was threshing with us on a farm at Hempstead, we were there on the Friday and the following Monday and Tuesday. On the Friday when we finished Jiver asked the farmer if he could have his day's pay so he gave him his money. When we finished on the Tuesday Mr Farmer came and paid the odd hands their three days pay and he also paid Jiver three days forgetting about paying him on the Friday. When we came away I heard some shouting, of course, the farmer had remembered he had paid Jiver too much. He said, 'I'll get it next time you come.'
Jiver, who was riding in the straw pitcher said, 'I shan't come na more.'
I don't think he ever did go there again.

When Rosie died he went from bad to worse. I called to see him I saw what should have been a chest of draws in his living room. The drawers were gone, Jiver had chopped them up for sticks. I noticed a broken window with ivy growing through, it was growing up the stairs. At the finish the poor old fellow was put in a home at Wroxham, I think he died there.

There was another fellow who went with us cutting bonds, he was good at that job, he couldn't speak very well, he was always dressed in rags his name was Billy Jickells, we always called him Monkey.

One day he was on top of the drum and he had busted the crotch out of his trousers, so everytime he stooped his private parts hung out, so I put the tube brush up and blacked them up. Old Billy swore and shook his fist at me.

Billy was put into an old peoples' home somewhere away and as far as I know that is where he died.

Another fellow who spent a lot of time with us was Jack Bugg who lived at Catfield, he was a funny chap he could work all right but if he got in a pub and had a few drinks he wanted to fight everybody, he was always called Trotter.

Jack Warnes, who lived at Hickling, was cousin to my mother he drove a threshing outfit for Kirby of Martham. When he finished with them at the age of seventy two he came with me, he was a marvellous man he was as tough as my Grandfather, who was his Uncle. He was with me at Catfield Hall when he put his hand in the baler to give the coulder a push one of the feeder rakes caught his hand, I saw the blood running so I said, 'What have you done now!'
He said, 'Thas nothen.'

I asked the foreman if he would take him to the doctors, which he did, and I think he put sixteen stitches in his hand. He was off work for the rest of the season but come the next harvest Jack was back.

He told me he was driver on a fishing boat out of Yarmouth when he was eighteen. He was the youngest driver to go from Yarmouth. He worked until he was about eighty.

Old John Risborough, who drove for Worts of Sutton Mill, took the children who attended the Baptist Chapel at Stalham, to Eccles beach. When John got there he cleared off to The Star at Lessingham and stopped there until they turned him out well oiled. By the time he got back they were ready to return home. His mate had kept the fire going, they hadn't got far when the old engine started to prime he smothered everybody with sooty oily water so everyone got off and walked home they wouldn't ride any further, he didn't get that job again.

Jimmy Kerrison, who was his steersman, told me when they stopped to pick up water at Ingham the old engine only had thirty pound of steam on. It was a big eight horse Marshall with six foot six inch wheels on the back.

John was a blacksmith by trade, he never was much of an engine driver, he could never start that engine in fast gear without the front wheels jumping off the road. I remember him well, he always wore a beard and he always had a wide awake hat on his head. He drove Hudson Barber's engine when his son Jack was ill, when he went up to the drum to pull it back he opened up when he should have stopped because the starting lever went opposite to what he was used to and pushed the front blower in.

Another man who did at one time feed the drum for Worts was a good beer drinker, his name was Charlie Chettleburgh, he was a big strong man his sons brought him in the Windmill pub at Sutton on his eightieth birthday and he drank more rum than a lot of younger men could drink and he walked out as if he hadn't had a drop.

Two more lovely old fellows who lived and worked in Sutton were Aaron Salmons he was

Ralph Buckenham cleaning the Clayton Double Crank Compound Engine. Standing next to my Burrell 'Prince Charles'.

the skep and basket maker, he had his own Osier Carr where he grew his own material for his trade. Aaron had a squeaky voice. Another old fellow lived opposite in what was called Scotland Yard, his name was Dick Knapp, he was the local mole catcher, he had a gruff voice. One night when they were coming home from the Windmill pub Aaron apparently weren't feeling too well, he said in his squeaky little voice, 'I think I'm gorna die Dick.' Then Dick, in his gruff voice replied, 'You ont die Aaron, yew hent done nothin wrong.'
This conversation was overheard by a neighbour.

Another man who was part of the village was Walter Gales the boot and shoe maker he would be in his little workshop knocking away when we went passed on our way to school. Later on another young man named Maurice Baker started doing boot and shoe repairs, he was living on the outskirts of the village. He was handicapped and always had to use crutches. I knew him well, he was a good tradesman, he was also a good darts player, we had some good games in the Catherine Wheel public house which was the meeting point in the village. Everything was organised in the Wheel. Football teams would be picked, anything to do with sport was done there. Of course, the old place have been closed for years, it is a private house now.

There was at one time three pubs in Sutton, the White Horse near the church have been closed for years, in fact I don't ever remember it being open. My Grandfather lodged there when he first came to work at Sutton, the other two are also shut now.

At one time there was two brick works in Sutton one was at Mill Farm but the one I remember best was on Hickling Road. Bob Baker and I have been there sometimes and scratched our initials on some bricks before they were baked. I think they made bricks there until the late 1920's, of course bricks were made at Ingham until the out-break of War.

I can still remember who lived in every house in Sutton when I was a boy, now I don't know anyone only the olduns, the place is full of strangers.

I could see and hear the railway engines when we lived in the railway carriages, I would have liked to drive one of them. I would spend a lot of time up at the station when they were shunting in the goods yard I would also get talking to the fellows on the engines, a lot of them lived in the Melton Constable area. I had hopes at one time of getting a job on the railway when I left school but there was no hope of that so I had to keep to traction engines.

I liked to see the trains going through on a Saturday morning full of people from the North and Midlands all off on holiday to Great Yarmouth sometimes with two engines in front.

We have recently bought the land where the station once stood, a new road is where the railway line used to be. I stood there only the other day and imagined I could hear those engines pulling out of the station.

CHAPTER EIGHT

SUTTON SALE AND LOCAL FAIRS

Every autumn a sale was held on a field in the village, it was called Sutton Trot, it was always at Michaelmas time and always on a field as near possible to the Windmill public house. This event was very popular with the local farmers and farm workers. The sale was made up with farm impliments of all descriptions including horses. I can remember a man who worked for Jonathan Howletts, the Auctioneers, running round with these horse putting them through their paces as they were being sold, his name was Nes Bell. This annual event carried on until the outbreak of War.

When I was at school a man by the name of Underwood, better known as Rhubard always came with his fairground amusements, it didn't amount to much. He had swinging boats, a coconut shy, a rock stall plus a few side stalls also another thing all decorated with mirrors they called Housey Housey. I seem to remember it was sort of a bingo game I know prizes were given, all these things were painted in bright colours so us kids thought it was wonderful.

The only means of transport were horses that pulled everything. Stall holders also came with all the usual stuff, it was a miniture market. I remember some fellows coming one year with a covered in lorry full of bicycles all sizes, Mr Baker, my mates father, bought Bob a new one it cost about one pound ten shillings. I know I was envious because my bike had a wooden seat and blocks on the pedals so I could reach them.

The pub was always full up, some of the old boys would have too much to drink I have seen some of them rolling about. A cockle stall would be on the pub forecourt. Most of the farm workers in this area would have time off work, some would get arguing about horses etc., and sometimes there was a fight.

When I was a wee lad I remember buying some thing from a stall priced three pence, I gave the woman in charge my sixpence, it was all I had, she gave me ninepence change, I disappeared right quick. After the stall holders had packed up and gone we would hunt about where the stalls had been, sometimes we would find a pencil, I think one boy found a shut-knife, it was all good fun.

Of course at Ingham, the adjoining village, a fair was held every year the week after Whitsun it was a much bigger fair than Sutton.

Us lads would shout and sing, 'Tomorrow is Ingham Fair I hope you'll all be there, fill your guts with monkey nuts and pints and pints of beer'.

In the morning of the first day there would be a bullock sale, farmers from miles around would be there, the Swan public house had a load of beer come in for the occasion, there was plenty of fighting going on there. Kenny Gray would be there with his steam horses and cake-walk and various other amusements but I was more interested in his engines. He had a Fowler Showman and a Garrett Showmans Tractor, they would all be polished up the electric lights would all be shining bright. It was marvellous to us boys because we had no electricity in those days.

There used to be a Mr Dack come with his amusements, I think he had a Burrell engine. A man by the name of Lenny Cardy drove Gray's Fowler, he was a good driver. When he left they had all sorts of drivers, old Kenny Gray would have a go himself, he never was much of a driver. Donald, his son, told me every time he did a journey on the road he ran the fuseable plug out, Donald drove the Garrett Tractor. He told me his father sent him to get the Fowler one day when he arrived the old man gave him some nasty looks because he had got the engine back without any trouble, I suppose he didn't like to think the boy was a better man then himself.

A few years later Kenny was heading for Yarmouth fair when disaster struck. He was driving the Garrett tractor which finished up broadside over in a big water dyke alongside the Acle straight I remember cycling over there one Sunday morning to see two of Thurstons Burrells pull it out, that was the finish of Kenny driving engines. George Thurtle a threshing contractor at Great Ormesby bought the Garrett repaired it and took all the Showmans fittings off and used it for threshing, a man by the name of Tom Carter drove it for him until diesel tractors came on the scene and then the Garrett was scrapped.

Ingham Fair was carried on after the War, Mrs Gray could always make some lovely rock. She was a very nice lady, I knew Donald very well he would sometimes stop at my place and have a look at my engines. The last time we met was at Wells, Donald had a Gift Shop there.

Every year Gray's held a Fair at Ludham, another nearby village, another man from Norwich with some stalls was always in attendance with Gray, his name was Summers. On one occasion when Gray's were moving from Ludham to Albourgh near Cromer their Fowler Engine came along and stopped at our engine yard gate, the driver came in and said he had just had a calamity. The nuts had become loose that held the gland on the high pressure piston rod the gland came off the crosshead hit it and broke both lugs off. This fellow had never drove the engine before. He was a big man, I should think he weighed about eighteen stone and he was swearing like a trooper, that didn't suit Grandfather at all as he was a religious man. Anyway, they shaped a flat peice of metal over the rod and held it in position by the two studs, of course, all the packing was gone. Ted repacked the gland and put locknuts on so everything went okay. Old Gray never did come and pay for the job.

After fixing them up they travelled on their way but they didn't get far when they got to Bengate bridge about two miles from North Walsham, the fellow ran the engine short of water and of course blew the fusible plug. A man who lived nearby told me they took the ash pan off and fire bars out and the driver was in the firebox taking the plug out, remember the engine was still hot. When Kenny Gray arrived on the scene he said he had never heard a man swear like it. He said this driver crawled out from under the firebox and the sweat was streaming off him. They told me he got to Albourgh late that night and packed the job up. I never did know his name but I think he came from the Deopham area.

George Plummer of Stalham was Jack of all trades. He had a saw yard also he was a haulage contractor, I always got on very well with him. On his land he would let the fair people pull in and sometimes have a small fair going. I remember Bert Stocks was there one week-end with his Burrell Princess Mary, a 7 h.p. engine, I think he had a set of dodgems. They were busy and that engine was barking well, her smoke box door was glowing red half way up. The engine is still in Norfolk.

A fellow from Yarmouth had a set of Gallopers complete with Savage Centre engine in Mr Plummer's yard, it was about the time when all the showmen were going in for modern rides, he built it up and had it going. I had an hour or two driving the engine for him one evening, he would have sold me the whole turnout. I sometimes think I should have bought them.

Thurstons of Norwich had some nice engines, a fellow who worked with us threshing went away and worked for Thurstons, he worked on the rides when they were in action and steered 'Unity' one of their engines when they were moving from one site to another. The driver of this engine was Harry Yull, he drove for Thurstons many years.

All these engines are restored and are in George Cushing's museum at Thursford. The Garrett engine which is there was new to Lacons the brewers of Yarmouth, they also farmed Hall Farm Mautby. Rampa Read drove it when it was new, he cut one of his fingers off in the gearing, when he finished Charlie Dove drove it. Charlie became landlord of a pub in Ormesby. Another young chap by the name of Lenny Kirk drove the Garrett for a short time, he then drove for George Barrett. Charlie then took Lacon's engine again. When George Thurtle bought the turnout he drove for him. After Charlie retired a fellow by the name of Billy Smith drove it, I knew all these men well.

CHAPTER NINE

WHEN THINGS BEGAN TO CHANGE

EARLY IN the 1950's I could see that the combine harvester was going to take over from threshing, a lot of the bigger farmers had already bought them also a contractor near me was running one so I thought I had better do something about it otherwise I looked like being left behind. I could see that all the money threshing contractors had spent updating their machines was money down the drain. All of us old threshing blokes had given our engines away scrap price, thousand of engines were sold for £15.00 each. I sold one for £10.00. We spent money putting our other machinery on pneumatic tyres, we bought diesel tractors and now I could see that they would soon all be obsolete, our livelyhood was slipping away. We didn't get any help from the Government either, not like I notice some sections of the community get. So I managed to buy a Massey Harris 726 Combine, I drove it myself and I did quite a lot of work with it. I had another man working for me and he drove my threshing set. Roy Dixon, my regular driver, was busy with his turnout. Roy didn't want anything to do with combines. He was threshing on a farm where there had been some combining done, this particular farmer was always shouting about something so he said, 'Roy, your laying down cloths aren't very big.' we always laid cloths down under and beside the drum.
Roy he said, 'I reckon they are as big as ones that were under that combine you had here.'
Mr Farmer had no answer to that.

The following harvest I bought another Massey. More and more people wanted their corn done in this way instead of having all the trouble of cutting and carting and threshing so I began to get more work than I could keep up with. We did still have enough threshing to do to last all winter but I could see the interest was turning to combining so the next summer I bought combine number three.

I also had to buy the property which I hired and lived in as my landlord had died. The only trouble was I hadn't any money left to buy it with, so I had to borrow some more money. I worked hard and repaid all the money I had borrowed so within two years the place was mine. It only cost a fraction of today's prices but it was a lot when you haven't got any. So owning my own place I could go to the bank with a bit more confidence. I also bought a new pick up baler, I then bought a new reversible plough and a new tractor, also a sugar beet harvester for contract work.

My eldest son, Malcolm, had left Grammer School and was working in an accountants office in Norwich, I thought he had chosen a better career than I ever had brains enought to do, but I was surprised when he said he wanted to work for me, I told him not to be so soft because if he came with me he would have to go threshing. It was no good of me talking he had made his mind up, so he came with me. I was still driving a threshing set myself so I put him on top of the drum bond cutting, I thought that will sicken him he will be glad to get back in that office but he didn't give in he stuck it out all through the winter. The next harvest I bought another combine and Malcolm drove it. I was by now employing five men. I also bought a crop sprayer and did quite a bit of spraying corn crops. I never did like that job so after a few years I gave up spraying and left that job to Hubert Sands, he specialised in that sort of work. Today he has one of the largest spraying and chemical handling companies in the business, they also build self propelled sprayers which are sold all over the British Isles. Hubert is about the same age as I am. I knew him when he was as hard up as I was but he has done very well in business.

In 1957 I bought my first new Claas combine, it was a marvellous machine it did the work of two of the old ones, it cost £2332. It was the same year the Royal Show was held in Norfolk at the Costessey showground.

The next summer I bought another new Claas combine and another pick up baler, the combine was the same price as the one the previous year, 'no inflation then'.

I was now running two beet harvesters, I think I was one of the first to lift suger beet on contract with a machine in the area. I bought a new space drill so I could also drill the seed. So still with some threshing and combining, spraying, drilling, beet harvesting and ploughing I had a full-time job but I still was not satisfied.

I bought a petrol tank which had been taken out at the garage at Repps, it was only a three hundred gallon tank which I thought would do my job, I thought if I bought my petrol in bigger lots I would get it cheaper. I cleaned the tank and had it tested, I then give it a coat of paint. One Sunday morning a customer called to see me, as we were talking he asked me what I intended doing with the tank. I then told him what I had in mind. He said he wondered if I was going in for selling petrol. I said I didn't suppose I would get permission to sell petrol here, I expected I would get too much opposition from the local garages. No, I didn't think that would work. After this conversation I couldn't get this petrol business out of my head, the more I thought about it the more interested I got. So I got in touch with one or two petrol companies, they soon sent their representatives to see me. I found one company was prepared to help me better than the others as regard finance. So planning was applied for, I then had highways people to see me then the police had to have a look. At the finish I began to get a bit fed up and thought I hope they don't pass it, but permission was given. I suppose it was to be.

I then got the finances sorted out and then everything started to happen. Two new five hundred gallon tanks arrived, I then removed a tree which stood in the way and then we started digging holes to put these tanks in. Malcolm and a fellow called Forder Plummer, his name was George, dug the holes with spades the tanks were then buried in sand, the pumps arrived and were fitted, I had the forecourt concreted, I built a kiosk with windows and sections I bought at a Government sale on Rackheath airfield. I fitted the place with shelves and bought a small till hoping we would take some money to put in it. A traveller called and said he could stock us up with car polish and dusters and all the stuff a motorist needed and pay when he called the next month he would then stock up again, I thought the very fellow I am looking for.

So Easter 1958 we opened for business. The first day I sold fourteen gallons, it was an uphill struggle for a start. I was selling Fina petrol the same as we are today as it was a new brand to the area I heard all sorts of comments. Our customers began to increase because we were open from early morning until late at night when the other filling stations were closed.

It amused me to hear some people say their car didn't run very well on Fina. One customer said he got a smell from it, some said their motor would not run on it at all, but I knew that the best grade that we were selling was picked up from a well known company in Yarmouth, so the petrol their car couldn't run on was exactly the same stuff as they were buying up the road.

Birds Eye were having a lot of peas grown in the area so I thought I would buy a pea cutter, I hadn't really got any work organised for this machine it was just a shot in the dark, mind you I let as many people as possible know I had bought it. Almost straight away Birds Eye were inquiring about doing some cutting as they were getting behind with the harvesting. We were then working away until the peas were all finished. The next season a group was formed in the Stalham area and I did all the cutting. I bought three more cutters, the farmers bought the loaders and I was in charge of the whole operation. I also bought two lorries and fitted them with tipping gear for carting peas to the vineries. My second son, Tony, said he wanted to work at home as he had been with another firm of agricultural engineers in Norwich for five years. I think they were disappointed as he was getting a handy chap, so he came and worked for me and was a big help on this pea job.

Malcolm, my eldest son, had to leave and do his National Service. He spent most of his time in Germany in the Royal Corps of Signals, it wasn't a waste of time as he learned typing also the German language which have come in very useful since we started doing business with the Germans. About the same time I somehow developed pleurisy and I hope I never have it any more and I don't wish it on anyone else, I thought at one time I was a gonna. When I thought I was getting better I got out of bed and came downstairs but when I wanted to go up again I thought I would never make it. I was a long time getting over it, in fact I don't think I could ever work the same as I had done in the past.

The two lorries I had were painted and looked smart, I made name boards and fixed them on top of the cab so everyone knew they were mine. I got the licence through without much bother, in those days it was A for a full licence B restricted milage or C for own use only, I got two Bs. The first morning we started carting I got them away about half past five in the morning and before six o'clock the telephone rang, and I was told one of my lorries was involved in an accident near Aylsham. I thought this is a good start, so away I went to have a look, Tony went with me. When we found the lorry it was wedged in with another lorry in a narrow road it did look a mess. I asked my driver what happened, he said he saw the other fellow coming and stopped because he knew there was not enough room to pass but the other lorry was coming too fast to stop. The back axle was knocked back, the body was smashed up completely. A man I knew who lived nearby came with a tractor and pulled the lorries apart, I sent Tony home to get some jacks and spanners etc. I managed to get the axle back into the right position it had sheared the rivets off the spring hangers, I bolted it back on and loaded all the broken woodwork onto our truck and drove it home. We got into work and stripped everything off the chassis. I rang the insurance company and told them. The man who I spoke to said they would have to send an inspector out and assess the damage, I told him I wanted to get the thing back on the road as soon as possible. So after telling him I could repair it myself he agreed for me to get on with the job and send them the bill. I managed to salvage one cross member in bits for a pattern. I measured up the wood for the floor boards etc., and went to Taylors of Wroxham where they cut out a set of cross members and loaded all the other timber onto my truck and away I came home and got into work.

Tony and myself rebuilt the lot and by nine o'clock that night it was ready to go. My night driver was there so he went to the pea field and got a load and was at Upton Vineries by midnight. We were working twenty four hours a day until the season was finished, the men worked a twelve hour shift but I have done thirty six hours without a break. Tony would keep going until he was tired out.

I then realised I hadn't a shed big enough to store my combines in during the winter so I had a new building put up big enough to put four Claas Combines in I also built another smaller one to put the balers in.

I had by this time started in the Plant Hire business, I bought a new Whitlock Dinkum Digger, I was one of the first in the area to hire those machines out, I soon had more work than I could do with one so I bought another and another and another. That is how it went on until I found I was running sixteen diggers.

Malcolm had by now finished his National Service so he did a lot in the office also he drove a lorry in the pea season. He would always get an extra load in more than the other drivers.

John, my third son, was getting busy with the petrol pumps and puncture mending. He also had a few chickens in the garden, he loved attending to them. We also installed a diesel pump and a two stroke pump to cater for motor bikes. We had started selling tyres and batteries so it was keeping him busy. I remember coming home from the pea field about two o'clock in the morning to find two lorries waiting for petrol so I switched the lights on and served them, then two more came in I was busy for a time then some fellow came in with a car. He said, 'Two please.' it struck me funny, I suppose he thought it was common practise for us to be open all night. I took his money and bade him goodnight.

We had by now a lady working full-time in the office. I had a new office-cum-stores measuring twenty feet by ten feet, at least it moved the paper work off the front room table. Malcolm then took charge of all office work. Tony was kept busy on repairs to our own machines, we then employed another fitter.

A man came in one day and said he represented a firm of importers and he thought I had a good chance of selling machines. I was a bit doubtful but on second thoughts I ordered some cage wheels and one cultivator. When these things were delivered I thought to myself what have I done now with all the other firms about dealing in agricultural machinery what chance have we got here. I needn't have worried. I sold them straight away, I ordered some more and sold them also and that was the start of dealing in machinery which has grown into big business.

I then had a farmer come along and said he wanted to buy a bigger combine as he was getting behind with his harvest and he had asked one or two dealers and they couldn't get him one so I telephoned a man I knew at Saxham in Suffolk and he told me there was only one in the coutry not sold and that stood on the docks at Harwich and if I wanted it he would send it home the next day. I rang the farmer and told him the news and he agreed to have it so it was deliver the next day. That was the start of selling combine harvesters. I took his small machine in part exchange and sold it almost straight away to another local farmer. Since then we have sold hundreds of combines and pick up balers.

The car repair business began to grow so I employed a mechanic and a young lad to help him to work full-time on cars, these two are still with us and very good men they are. We now have eleven car mechanics.

I soon realised we would have to build a new workshop so I got in touch with two firms and selected one and after plans were passed and prices were sorted out we moved into the combine shed for a workshop using one end as stores. We then demolished all the old buildings and had this steel framed and brick building put up which was big enough for two offices, a showroom, workshop and stores. However, we found that trying to repair cars and tractors in the same building was not the right thing to do. We then began to look over the fence for more space. Behind our place was a small field of about two acres. This land was owned by an estate controlled by a firm of agents in Norwich. I contacted these people about possible purchase but could get nowhere with them. As time went on my son Malcolm became friendly with a young fellow then starting in business as an estate agent so he mentioned it to him about this land, he said he could try and negotiate with these people. I said go ahead by all means which he did very successfully, we went ahead and bought the land at what seemed a very high price at the time, of course, if we hadn't we would never have had another chance. We moved on as soon as the farmer had cleared mangels off. We then built new stores and offices and applied for planning consent to build new workshops and concrete the surrounding area, complete with washing down pad and loading ramp.

We built agricultural workshops on our new site, which have been in use now several years, we also bought the farm house and buildings adjoining our premises and demolished the buildings and made a new entrance. We are about to turn the farmhouse into a lawn mower and garden machinery department with showroom. Everything now is done through a computer. The motorists shop stocks all the necessary bits and pieces, chocolates, sweets and cigaretts, are all sold there. I was asked one day what we sold, I said everything from a Mars Bar to a combine harvester.

I had in my spare time, which wasn't a lot, hired ten acres of land at Stalham and farmed it until it was sold for building a housing estate known as Heron Gardens, I don't know where they got the Heron bit from. It was a very good piece of agricultural land and I was sorry to lose it.

About the same time a man who I knew very well asked me if I wanted to buy a four acre field at Sutton, I said why not, so I had another deal. We farmed it a few years and I then received a letter from Norfolk County Council Education Committee to say they would like to buy part of this field to build a new school. I knew a new school was in the pipeline because I was at that time a school manager at Sutton. So after a bit of negotiating I sold it.

About the same time a little farm at Catfield came on the market. The house had been damaged by fire, a new poultry house had been built and it was fitted with battery cages all automatic but the fellow had neglected everything. When I bought it the cages were full of dead hens and there was muck on the floor six inches deep I had never seen such a mess we had a lovely job cleaning that lot up. There was also a piggery which would hold about one hundred and twenty pigs.

Anyway, after buying this place I was working there and it struck me what a lovely quiet place it was. I said to my wife if I built a new house there it would be a nice place to live. She agreed but said it is lonely and further away from shops etc. Anyway, we did just that, we built a new bungalow and mother learnt to drive a car so everything worked out well. So after thirty years we moved from Stalham Green and the house where we started our married life and raised eight sons and six daughters, all are alive and kicking.

We have now lived at Staithe Farm twenty years. We have planted trees and shrubs everywhere, our drive is lined with flowering cherry and mountain ash, it is very colourful all through the summer.

About twenty five years ago I bought two small muck spreaders and soon found there was an opening for that sort of work so the next year I bought two bigger ones. I then bought a crawler tractor and made a big fork to load the muck. I sold the small spreaders and bought two more big machines and then we were in the spreading job properly with a gang of four men on piece work, they really did shift the muck. We are still in the spreading business of course the spreaders are bigger than ever now.

A farmer telephoned me one evening and asked me if I could drill some wheat for him I said I could. I then thought I don't know how as I hadn't a drill, so I rang Ernest Couzens who was a machinery salesman and told him I wanted a second-hand drill. He picked one up from a farm the next day and brought it to me. I found out he hadn't even had a deal with the man the drill belonged to. Anyone who knew Ernest will believe this. He then went round and sold the other man a new one and I kept the old one.

I asked Ernest one day if he had a second-hand combine to sell me he said there was one standing on a farm at Truch so I went and collected this machine and put it straight to work he phoned and asked if I had been to have a look at this machine, I said I've collected it and it is working, he said he hadn't had a deal with the farmer yet so he had better get round there quick, which he did and sold him a new one.

CHAPTER TEN

OUR FAMILY

I MUST STOP writing about things I have done or have not done and tell you a little about our children who my wife and myself are very proud of.

I know I started the business and we both worked very hard and laid the foundations for what is now a big business and turning over millions of pounds. I still think sometimes of the days when I was cranking about on a bike in all weathers daubed up with muck and grease. My sons all work hard and a lot of the credit must go to them. They are all shareholders, six of them are directors, they have all got their individual jobs to do. I put them all in charge of something, of course, they don't take too much notice now of what I say, I sometimes get told to bugger off. This I do gladly.

Malcolm is Boss Man, more or less over the lot. He has a good business brain, can price a job for the plant hire side, such as land leveling or ditching and in the next breath talk finance with a finance company or anything else that comes along. He is never lost for words, I have seen more than one Government Inspector of various departments come into his office very big and important people go away with their tail between their legs.

Tony, my second son is up to his neck in machinery. He can sell ice cream to an eskimo, he is never happy only when he is having a deal, either tractor, combine or a baler. I should think he knows what make of tractor every farmer in Norfolk has got. He also farms a piece of land and he lives in a lovely old farm house in sight of our works. I tell him sometimes he works and worries too much. He will help anyone out of a muddle, a lot of the farmers who he has helped don't always appreciate the help he has given them.

John, my third son, is in charge of the garage. He is also a worker, he is always at work before seven in the morning and he organises the car repair side also accident repairs, insurance jobs etc. He has a nice house in Brumstead Road, Stalham. I tell him sometimes I wouldn't do his job I would not have the tolerance to stand and listen to some of the people when they come in grumbling about their bills and everything else they can find to moan about.

Roger, my fourth son, is stores manager, he does all the buying for the stores. He sort everything out such as discounts, which have to be watched very closely. He started his working life in the grocery trade. He lives on the premises in his own house. He is not so firery as the three older ones, takes after his mother, but if he do get angry he can be very nasty.

Henry, my fifth son, is in charge of agricultural spares, he is the family comedian, always cracking a joke about something. I have heard customers say that they like coming to our stores just to see Henry. His first name is Gordon but he is known by everyone as Henry. He is a very

Great Grandfather Jesse born at Salhouse 1832—died at Sutton 1918.

busy man and lives in a bungalow in Brumstead Road. He learnt his trade in the stores with another firm in Norwich. He says all sorts of things to some of those farmers. One day a customer who grows strawberries came in for two bolts so Henry served him and booked them out, Mr Farmer said 'You are never going to charge me for two bolts are you!'
Henry said, 'Of course I am, you don't give me any of your strawberries.'

Alan, my sixth son, is foreman in the agricultural workshops, he started working in the business straight from school, he is Jack of all trades, he can turn his hand to anything. He is very neat and tidy in everything he do, he is another placid sort of fellow. He lives in his own bungalow at Catfield.

David, my seventh son, is now a fitter on the agricultural side, he is the baler specialist. He loves balers, he will work all night if necessary to get one going. He started his career with a frozen food company. He also owns a bungalow at Sutton. He is a level headed chap, the others don't upset him because he was at one time a boxer. He had to retire because of a broken jaw which happened playing football.

Timothy, our youngest son, works on the sale side of the lawn mower department. He started with the company when he left school. He was petrol pump attendant, but after a time he got fed up with that. He does quite a bit of selling and organises repairs on garden machinery. He owns a house in Sutton.

The girls are all married. Doreen, our eldest, is the wife of a farmer living in Suffolk. She is always busy doing something. She was a hairdresser, she did at one time work for one of the top hairdressers in London.

Margaret, our second daughter lives in the Norwich area. She has been in nursing for over twenty five years. She is now a Nursing Sister and a District Nurse. Her husband is with the Gas Board.

Beryl, our third daughter is the wife of a Hotelier she also does part-time in a Norwich store.

Carol, our fourth daughter, works in a bank at Stalham. Her husband is workshop foreman in our car workshop. They are now building themselves a new house at Ingham.

Judy, daughter number five, is also a nurse at a hospital in Norwich. She works in an operating theatre. Her husband is a Police Officer.

Christine, our youngest, was also a hairdresser but at the moment is living in Germany as her husband is serving in the R.A.F. over there. Christine and her husband, John, were driving along one of the autobahns in Germany when they were stopped for speeding. The young speed cop was very nice about it all but fined them fifty marks and said 'Be careful, and drive more fastly.' I wonder what some of our policemen would say if they had to speak German.

We have at present got thirty seven grandchildren and one great grandchild.

I was very lucky to have married a woman like my wife she is a wonderful woman. She is the one who brought our family up as I was always working away from home, at one time I hardly ever saw my house in day light except on Sundays. The children were always clean and well dressed and always well fed.

Things were always done in rotation, they would have a little packet of sweets on Tuesdays and again on Saturday, they never asked for anymore. They were always off to bed when tea was over until they got older. School clothes came off as soon as they were home and they were never allowed to run on the road after school. When mother said no it meant no. They all did a turn at washing up the crockery and other little jobs, of course they were awarded a few pence. I am pleased to say they have all made respectable citizens.

We have no children living with us now. We are Darby and Joan. I sometimes tell my wife she expects me to eat as much as all them children did, she can't get used to cooking for two.

I have taken her on several business trips abroad and have stayed in some lovely hotels which she enjoyed.

After we had been at Stalham a few years and our family was getting bigger we decided to have a new kitchen built with a new bedroom on top. It was a big help as we now had four bedrooms also we had a new electric cooker so it was out with the old wall oven. We were still a bit cramped but we managed. There was no central heating in them days, not for us anyway. My wife would keep the little ones warm with hot water bottles.

She did the children's washing every day, I have seen her getting nappies off the line frozen stiff and her hands were very cold. When I hear some of the squit there is today about bring children up I think of those days long ago. We had no family allowance only for the younger ones, which was only a few shillings a week but it was very acceptable.

When the children were small we would have some fun at some of the things they used to say. When Tony and John were young they dug theirselves a little garden. I could hear them talking. Then Tony he called Doreen, my eldest daughter, and said 'How do you spell keep, I know how to spell out. T.O.U.' They were putting a sign up.

CHAPTER ELEVEN

HOLIDAYS AND TRIPS ABROAD

THE FIRST holiday we ever had was twenty five years after we were married. We had a week in Scotland, what a wonderful sight for the first time, all those mountains and hills. My wife was completely overcome she really enjoyed herself. We have been back many times since and stayed several times in Braemar. I was driving from the village up to the Lyn of Dee to see salmon leaping up stream, they really do jump out of the water. As we were going along this little road in the hills on a clear piece of land what did I see! I saw some threshing going on. I said to my wife, I must stop and have a look at this. I took some photos, one old fellow told me that they could get a frost up there every month of the year. He said, 'We are a bit too near the moon.'

We had a holiday in Norway, flying from Norwich Airport to Bergen. My wife is a member of the W.I. and they were organizing trips over there so we went and stayed at Ulvik, a little village on the Hardanger Fiord. We had several trips on the fiords and visited a lot of other places of interest. I didn't see any engines over there.

We were travelling on a coach to a town called Voss, we had to travel along an unmade up road, one of the rear wheels picked up a rock in between the twin wheels. The driver eventually stopped and tried to get this piece of rock out but he couldn't. Of course, I had to get out and have a look. The driver couldn't speak English so I said to the courier, tell him to loosen the wheel nuts then the rock will come out. She told him my suggestion in Norwegian language. He jabbered something. She then told me he said he couldn't do that as it would let the oil out. I won't tell you what my answer was. The name of the place we were stuck was 'Stalham'. Another coach appeared from somewhere so we all boarded that and left the other fellow to sort his wheel out. We found Norway a very nice country.

Another time we went on a factory visit in Ireland. We flew from Heathrow to Dublin and stayed in a first class hotel in Dublin. We went to Carlow beet factory, the Armer Sugar Beet Harvesters are also made there, everyone made us very welcome.

On the Saturday we were taken to the Leopardstown races, we had a V.I.P. lounge at our disposal everything we had was paid for by the owners of the beet factory, Erin foods. They were sponsoring the races that day. What amazed me was the number of priests having a flutter.

We were introduced to some of their members of Parliment. We had one or two in our party who made a fool of themselves they also got the coach driver drunk. How he got us back to the hotel safe I shall never know, my wife was not amused. We had three wonderful days.

A certain manufacturer of fork lifts which we were selling offered a holiday at a Castle in

ABOVE *My wife and myself with friends at Leopardstown races in Ireland in 1978.*
BELOW *A party off to the J.C.B. factory to see the machines made. I am on the right.*

Scotland to every dealer who had sold a certain number of machines. We had reached the target so my wife and myself went to Grantully Castle. We spent about four days there, it was a lovely place. Plenty to eat and drink, but the trouble was the Laird was on his own as his wife was in hospital, or so we were told. He had two students from Australia doing the cooking but they couldn't cook. We had partridge one night when they were cut open the blood ran out. We also had venison and salmon. Everything was raised on the estate. On the last night things were a lot better I shall never forget that meal, everything was done in style all the cutlery and candlelabras were pure silver, it was a wonderful sight. We were piped into the dining room with bagpipes, when we were seated the main course was also piped in.

We had two days groase shooting on a nearby estate, I didn't do much good at that, they flew too fast for me. We were standing in what they call butts on the side of them hills these birds would appear and disappear right quick. One afternoon we had a duck shoot, I did manage to get a pair of them. One man in the party had a bald head, the sun was shining bright so the keeper with him said, 'Put your hat on Sir your head is frightening the ducks away.'

This fellow with the bald head was standing in a butt with a keeper and a dog. They were about three down from me, I heard his gun go off, both barrells. He frightened the life out of the keeper and nearly shot his dog. They were brand new spanish guns. This fellow said it went off when he closed it, but the old Major in charge wasn't too happy. The Duke who owned the place said he wouldn't have the fellow there the next day, it could have caused a nasty accident.

Some of the party had a day's salmon fishing it was a lovely place we both enjoyed it, more so because everything was free. After all that rich food I said to my wife on the way home, I think we had better stop at a cafe so I can have a cheese roll, which I did, and believe me it was lovely.

We had a weekend in London and stayed at a hotel in the West End. On the Sunday we were walking round and found ourselves outside the Old Bailey Court House. As we stood outside a police officer looked out and said, 'Would you like to have a look round!' Of course, we accepted his offer. He showed us all the court rooms and also the cells underneath. One of the rooms we went in was where the last woman to be hanged spent her last night.

I did at one time always have a few days at the Smithfield Show at Earls Court. I have stayed at various hotels in that area. I arrived one year at the hotel I was booked in only to be told that they had doubled booked my room. I was told they had booked me a room round the corner. So I found this other place and left my case. When I returned that night I found I was the only Englishman there, I didn't mind that but when I found I had to share a room I wasn't too happy. The next morning I told them what they could do with their room and moved out.

Three of my sons and myself were on a flight to Hanover in Germany when the Captain warned us of turbalance when the plane suddenly lurched over just as a hostess was pushing her trolley up the gangway loaded up with the leftovers of a meal, it tipped over on top of some fellow who happened to be near. That was the roughest flight I ever had.

We had a coach holiday in Scotland which was very good but on the way home we stopped the night at a hotel in Newcastle when the luggage came up my wife's case was missing. Someone stole it, all her clothes were gone, it did upset her. I had a job to get the insurance money. They tried all sorts of excuses at the finish I got a bit upset about it and told them I would get my solicitor to deal with it. We did then get a settlement.

On another occasion I attended a convention held in Bavaria, Southern Germany, my wife also went, we stayed in a lovely hotel at a place called Schwangue which is at the foot of the Alps, it is a ski resort in winter. We went up the mountains in a cable car, mother didn't think much of that, I quite enjoyed it. You didn't realise the speed they travelled until you meet another car going like hell the other way.

I watched some of these fellows hang gliding from the top of these mountains there were platforms built on the slope. When they started running to take off there was no turning back they had to go, I don't think I would try that.

We also went another time and stayed in a big hotel beside a lake the place was Tegern See. All the hotels and houses were built with timber. They were all decked out with flowers, I had never seen such a sight. The first morning we were there was Sunday, I walked onto the balcony outside our room, the church bells were ringing across the lake and echoing in the mountains, it was marvellous. The whole place was so clean and tidy.

The convention which I was there to attend was held in a big timber building even that was decorated with geraniums growing everywhere. Early in the morning I saw men sweeping the roads, when they finished there wasn't a leaf out of place.

I went to Sweden to visit a factory making agricultural machinery. We were treated very well, after we finished our factory visit they arranged a visit to Finland on a ferry. It was on a Saturday night, the wind was blowing I had never had an experience like it. When we had left the shelter of the land the waves got bigger. Two thirds of the passengers were sea sick, I was for one. I had never felt so ill I didn't think I would live long enough to see Finland. I stood on the side deck with a friend when a wave broke over us, I was hanging on the rail the water went in the top of my neck and came out of the legs of my trousers. I was sure the boat was about to sink.

I noticed over there if the pedestrian lights were red nobody crossed the road, it is an offence and anyone who disobeyed are fined. Also the motorists had head lights on all day. Their speed limits are strictly obeyed.

I also visited a factory in Italy, near Rome. I went in the Vatican, it is a wonderful building. Rome is a lovely city, but the traffic is terrible.

The maddest place of the lot was Copenhagen, I did once spend three days there to see some new tractors announced. The pubs are open all night on Saturdays, I have never seen so many young people drunk.

We have visited several cities in Germany and found them all clean and tidy and all the people very helpful and friendly.

CHAPTER TWELVE

ODDS AND ENDS

DURING THE War an order came out from the War Agricultural Committee that all stacks of grain had to be surrounded by wire netting while it was being threshed. The mesh to be not more than one inch, fixed firmly with stakes to stop all vermin from escaping. So the contractor doing the job had to provide a set of iron stakes and the netting and were responsible for erecting it every day. This was a good idea, we had to supply all this, put it up to stop rats which the farmer had been feeding, they weren't our rats. Anyway, when we finished we had to take it down roll it up pack it away. All this was done free of charge as far as the engine owner was concerned. If we failed to do this we were prosecuted. They expected us to kill the rats as well, but that didn't very often come off.

I was threshing at Ludham one morning, things weren't going too well the top of the stack was wet and grown, that meant corn was coming out everywhere it shouldn't, all old engine men know what I mean. The man who was sacking corn said to me, 'Who is that fellow standing there?'

When I looked towards the engine there stood the man in blue. When I went over to him he said, 'Whose in charge here!'

I said to him that I was.

He then said, 'Where is your netting!'

I pointed to a roll of netting lying on the ground.

He said, 'It should be round that stack.'

I said, 'I know it should but I haven't had time to put it up.'

He was still running on about the fact that it should have been up before we started.

I said, 'Why don't you put it up, it don't seem as if you have got much to do.' He didn't like that so me and the farmer had to go to court at North Walsham. I was fined £1.00 and the farmer had to pay five shillings. Me and the farmer had a good day out.

The next time I saw the policeman was in the Windmill pub, he said, 'Well here is old Lord Wire Netting.' We had a drink together and finished up the best of friends.

My family had a painting done of me at work in my workshop. Malcolm came along with this man but he didn't tell me who he was he said he wanted to take some photographs of my models. He was a professional artist. They gave me a party for my seventieth birthday and presented me with the painting it was a complete surprise.

When I reached the age of seventy I was told one day I was wanted at Stalham at two thirty, so I made my way there and got another big surprise. I was called into the car showroom, I wondered what was going on as the place was full of workmen and office staff who had got to-

This is my model 'Burrell' 3″ scale engine, also model 'Garrett' drum.

gether and presented me with a pair of cut glasses inscribed with a traction engine and who they were from. I looked round all these people who worked for the company and some of my family. Some of these men had been with me for twenty five years. I had a lump in my throat when I said a few words of thanks and my mind went back to the first day I took the place over. I had taken a few of my belongings there on Charlie's pony and cart. Me and Roy Dixon had sat on the floor of the old workshop and ate our sandwiches forty eight years before. I remembered saying as we sat there, I don't know how long I'll be here the rent is high, we shall have to see how things go.

In the early days I would give Roy his money on the Saturday and I would sometimes borrow sixpence from him during the next week to buy a packet of cigaretts with. Roy retired when he reached the age of sixty five having worked for me forty six years. I knew when he finished he wasn't feeling too well but he would never tell you much. I called and saw him one day after he retired, he told me then he was not feeling up to much, I told him to see a doctor which he agreed to do. The next thing I heard he had died. He is buried in Happisburgh church yard. He was a very honest and conscienteous man and I missed him a lot when he finished.

I bought a little Devonshire type Burrell it was a single crank compound engine on springs, Roy drove it for a time but he didn't like it he would rather have a big engine.

During the War we had several prisoners of War helping us some were Germans but most of them were Italians. I would get talking to these fellows and we would make each other understand what we were talking about. Some of them were good men and they didn't want the War anymore than we did. Some would show me photographs of their wives and families and I have seen them crying while talking to me as their English was about as good as my Italian. I can remember one fellow making wooden toys for Christmas all he had for tools was a shutknife, I bought some of these things for my children for a shilling or two.

When I first had a Claus Baler to tie the straw behind the drum I was threshing for Jack Pestle at Hempstead his straw stacker was not used to stacking bunches when we were on the finish he had a hole in the top of the stack he wanted more straw to level the stack off but we hadn't got any more. Jack came in the field he said to me, 'What the hell has Basil been doing!'
I said 'What's up now.'
He said, 'That straw stack it looks more like Napoleons bloody hat.'

I often think of the things some of the old fellows used to say. George Thurtle of Ormesby who was a threshing contractor and engineer, he learned his trade at Burrells of Thetford. His saying was, 'There are two things you will never find in heaven, they are a Bald Donkey and a Satisfied Farmer.'

I was talking to Harry Bushell of Thursford who at one time was a threshing man, he ran five sets of tackle, he was a good friend of mine. I was telling him all the mistakes I had made he said, 'The man who never made a mistake never made anything.' The more I think of his words the more I think he was right.

I had another customer at Hoveton who always did his barley straight off the shock in the harvest. I had not had any money for doing all this so about November I biked there one evening it was six miles there and asked him if I could have some money. He said no he couldn't let me have any until I had finished the stacks which he had there. So I biked home again with no money. He paid when we finished the season after grumbling about the size of the bill, he was a

Scotsman. I did his work another few years he was a very hard man to deal with. The last harvest I did his threshing he couldn't get enough labour to do the job properly simply because he would not pay the price. We were working short handed, I was driving the engine and sacking chaff which can be a busy job. I did this for three days, he then said 'I hope you don't expect to get paid anything for the extra work, as you are charging enough already.'
I then told him I wouldn't look after the chaff anymore. So he took a man off the straw stack and put him on the chaff job. After a time he got wrong with one of his men on the straw so he took the fellow off the chaff again. So I said, 'Who is doing the chaff now!'
He said, 'You will have to.'
I told him I wouldn't do it anymore so he said, 'Ere, if you no like to do it you can pack up and go.'
I said right and got onto the engine and pulled the lever. Roy he looked round and said, 'What's up!'
I said, 'Sweep the drum down and pack it up.' which he did. So we hooked on and pulled out. It all happened in a very short time. He then came back and said if I would set the turnout again he would pay me to do the chaff, but I had other ideas and I told him what he could do with his chaff and his threshing. We came to Ludham and started there straight away on another farm.

Years later he telephoned me one night and asked me if I could do some pick-up baling for him, of course, when he asked the price it was too much. He said he knew another fellow who was cheaper, I told him he had better get the other man. I think there was a halfpenny difference. Anyway, he rang back the next day and said the other man couldn't come, I sent a baler there as soon as I could and he did eventually pay.

The first year I started on my own I took my engine and pulled trees and hedges out at Stalham for the late Mr Ivan Wright, every time I travel along the road from Stalham to Ingham and see that big feld I feel guilty and think how much nicer it would look with those trees there.

When John left school he had some poultry on our peice of land but fowl pest broke out in the area so they all had to be destroyed. The spare food he had lying about had to be buried in the garden. My cousin Jack also had a lot of poultry all his were destroyed. I knew Jack had some rats about there but nothing like we experienced one evening. I went outside and I couldn't believe my eyes there were rats everywhere, they were even up the apple trees eating the few apples that were left and eating the sprouts off the stalks in the garden. My wife went upstairs out of the way, she was scared. I had seen plenty of rats when I went threshing but nothing like I saw that night. Where John had buried the surplus food there was a heap of them all trying to get at it. I was afraid they would get indoors by this time we were all getting the wind up. I rang the council man also the Agricultural Committee, they were not very pleased because I was ringing them after hours. One said, 'Don't you know our office closes at five o'clock.'
I said, 'I can't help that I have a sworm of rats on my doorstep.' I did not go to bed that night, the next morning the rat catchers came and laid poison everywhere. By then most of the rats had gone but they came the next day and picked up one hundred and fifty dead ones. After that I got a good size bill for their work, I had to pay it though they were not my rats.

CHAPTER THIRTEEN

RESTORATION RALLIES AND MODELS

In the 1950's people started taking notice of 'them old engines' when most of them had been cut up and made into razer blades. Two fellows started all this rally business by having a race with two engines, it went on from there.

I remember going to Andover one day to see some engines in steam, I said to my cousin Tom, we must be going daft to run all this way to see an old engine after all the swearing I have done about them. On the way home we saw another one, a Garrett, it had steam on it was in a scrap yard. The man who owned it told us that a Burrell Showmans engine was at a fair in Braintree, so we had to go there and have a look at it. I am told it was sold for very little money.

Coming home through Sudbury Tom was driving my car he took the wrong road near a church, so he went round the church and got back on the right road to Bury St Edmunds. As soon as we were on the right road we were stopped by the police who said we had come along a one way street. I told him we had not been in the street and tried to explain to him what had happened. He said what had I got to do with it, I said it was my car but he would not listen he took Tom's name and address. I think he was fined £1.00.

About the same time I saw Mr Whipps of Woodton who had bought three or four engines and he said he had a Clayton and Shuttleworth for sale, just before that I bought 'Chronicals of a Country Works' by R. H. Clark. It was the history of Burrells of Thetford. The more I read and looked at the photos the more the bug began to bite. I thought don't be so daft Jimmy you don't want any more to do with them old things. Anyway, at the finish I went and bought the Clayton engine, a double crank compound on springs No: 47216. So one morning me and Roy went to Woodton and got up steam and drove it home to Stalham. It was in good order on top but I found the fire box wasn't too good so we cleaned it and painted it and I took it to the first engine rally ever to be held in Norfolk.

One day I was driving through Spixworth, two of my boys were riding with me, I said, 'That old Burrell that Tim Bullimore used to drive for Aldridge is about here somewhere'. I had heard it was being used for sterilising glass houses. One of the boys said, 'Look dad I can see a chimney up over that hedge.' So I stopped and had a look, I could then see it. So I turned the car round and drove down this little lane to this nursery. When we got a bit nearer I could see the engine standing there, it was as rusty as a horse shoe, it had stood seven years with no cover on. The owner of the place saw me, so I introduced myself and then I asked if he wanted to sell the engine. He said he had several people after it. I told him it was in a bit of a mess but I

ABOVE *Me and Tom at the Royal Norfolk Show with the turn out 1981.*
BELOW *The Fowler Roll which was in the film Swallows and Amazon.*

would give him seventy five pounds for it. The old boy thought for a minute and then said if I could find a boiler up to do his job I could have it. I got in touch with George Brooks, who was with Page of Sprowston who did a lot with boilers, and told him the tale, he said they had got the very thing. So George had a deal.

The first chance I got I went and steamed the engine up. The owners son came and had a look and told me what the levers and things were all for and explained how the thing went. I said yes and no. By this time she had about 120 pounds of steam on. He said he would have to go away for a little while. I had another man with me so we cleared all the debris and muck away and freed the steering worm, I put the old girl in gear and she jumped out there like a two year old and I stopped when I was on the hard road. When this young fellow came back his eyes nearly came out. He said, 'You have been having me on, you have driven one of them before.' I laughed and told him that I was driving one before he was born. He didn't have a lot more to say. We loaded it onto a low loader and brought it home.

I spent quite a lot of time and money on it. I still have it, I called it Prince Charles, it is a nice engine. I took it to a rally after we had repaired and painted it and a man came and spoke to me and said, 'They tell me this is the engine that stood at Spixworth'.

I said, 'That's right.'

He then went on to tell me he went and had a look at it and thought it was too far gone to have a go at.

Of course, since then some of these engines have been completely rebuilt from scrap. I then sold the Clayton, it is still around I saw a photograph of it in a book it is now called Lady Jane, sometimes I wish I hadn't sold it.

I went to the Woodton Rally once but for some reason I didn't take my engine. I suppose I had been busy doing something so there was no time to get the engine ready. As I was wandering around I met an old friend, Bob Shingles from Lingwood, who was a threshing contractor. Bob had driven all sorts of engines in his time doing haulage work also ploughing engines in Lincolnshire.

As we were having a yarn a man of the cloth, who was a vicar near Norwich said he did at one time work at Fowlers of Leeds, he came onto the rally field with a Fowler ploughing engine. Bob he looked at him and said, 'There look at that silly old bugger he should be teaching people to pray. He have got something there which will learn him how to swear if he is on there long enough.

I had a telephone call one day from a man working for the B.B.C. he said he had heard I had a steam roller, if so could I take it to Horning to appear in a film they were about to shoot in the broads area. The title was 'Swallows and Amazons' which was shown on B.B.C. 2. So on the appointed day I loaded the roll onto our low loader and Geoffrey, our lorry driver, took it to Horning. I unloaded it near the Swan Hotel about eight thirty, some of the people were already there, the people in charge rolled up about nine. Then a coach load came, there was also a coach full of costumes. The young lady who was helping to organise things said I had better change some of my clothes to old time dress, as the film was supposed to have been in older times. So I went in the bus where all these costumes hung. The young lady in there said I had better change my shirt and boots and wear another hat, an old fashioned cap. So I pulled my shirt off she handed me one of these old ones. I said, 'What about my trousers do you want me to take them off!'

She laughed and said, 'No, I think yours will do.'
I thought what a shame.

Another young lady said she thought I should have my hair cut. So I sat on a chair on the Swan car park and had a hair do. The next thing they were queueing up for breakfast from a mobile canteen. The lady in charge said, 'Come on Jimmy.' she had learned my name by now. I said, 'I've had mine.'
She said, 'Never mind have another one.' Which I did and had a full English breakfast.

By the time they wanted me to start operating it was time to stop for coffee and other drinks. When I did start I had to drive the roll up the road passed the cameras. I did this about a dozen times, I had to time this with some children running down a side road to see me go passed. By now it was lunch time so I joined the queue again and had another cooked meal.

After having a pint in the Swan the lady in charge said, 'I think we have finished with you now.'
I thought what a shame, I could put up with this for a week.

When the film was shown on television you could just see the roll go passed and that was it, but I did enjoy myself and I enjoyed it even more when I received a cheque for the job.

I have taken my Burrell engine with Ransome Drum and Straw Pitcher to the Strumpshaw Rally a few times. The Rally is organised by the Norfolk Steam Engine Club. I was Chairman for three years and quite enjoyed it.

I had a fellow come to me when I was looking after the engine there myself, who said, 'Do you know you are running your elevator the wrong way!'
I said, 'Do you think so!'
He said, 'Yes.'
I told him, 'Do you know old boy you have taught me something after me using a threshing set for thirty years, I never knew you ran the straw pitcher backwards.'
I knew he had got the pitcher mixed up with a corn elevator which did run the otherway round. He insisted he was right so I let him keep thinking.

The Fowler Steam Roller I bought from a man who at one time owned a big haulage and contracting business in Norwich. It stood behind his house, his children had it there to play with. It is a ten ton roll a double crank compound built 1923. It was in a sorry state when I bought it. Roy Dixon was with me then. We stripped it completely and rebuilt it. I did a lot of welding on it, new tubes, new axles and bearings. New slide valves, new canopy and lots of other jobs. After we painted and lined it she looked quite smart. I have built a shed at Staithe Farm large enough to hold all my machinery.

I always did say that when I reached retiring age I would build myself a model traction engine. So I bought a set of castings from Mr Plastow and some sheets of copper and I got into work. I also bought a set of drawings for a 3″ scale quarter size engine. I thought I would build a Burrell so I could make it look like my full size one. I made the boiler first and then the road wheels. So after three years of part-time working I produced an engine looking very much like my big one. I painted and lined it in the same colours. I entered it in the Model Engineers Society exhibition in Norwich and it was awarded a Bronze Medal. So I thought well it can't be that bad.

After that I went to Yarmouth with Jack Littleworth, a friend of mine, who is a retired Motor Engineer also a model maker and garage owner. Jack wanted to see a man who dealt in bits and pieces of tools and materials. In his store-cum-workshop I noticed a box full of castings and a part built boiler. I asked him what it was all for and he told me it was material for a Burrell Gold Medal Tractor 2″ scale, he also had a set of drawings, so I bought the lot. Now after working for nearly five years on it I now have a nice little double crank compound engine I have it standing in our hall on a little table and it looks really smart.

I have been working now for two years building a 3″ scale Garrett Drum.

Celebrating our Golden Wedding.

CHAPTER FOURTEEN

CONCLUSION

I HAVE now nearly ran out of steam and I hope that everyone who has read my book will have got some enjoyment from it. A lot of other people could have done the job better, I have written it exactly the way I remember it, as I said before I was never a brilliant scholar but I have done my best.

We enjoy living at Staithe Farm, we are surrounded with nature, the pheasants come all round our bungalow, we have every bird there is around us. I often see a heron in the dyke. In the spring I love to see the hares playing on the field sometimes there is roe deer running about.

My wife was taking Tessa, our dog, for a walk and saw about a dozen red deer in our neighbours field. I think they roam the marshes and woodland between Hickling and Horsey. Every year we have some wild duck nesting here also we have now got some foxes about. At night I can hear all sorts of animal and bird noises I think they all come here because they know they are safe.

I have a gun but never use it, also my wife always puts food out for the birds. If there is a shoot on locally we get plenty of pheasants and partridges, they know I won't hurt them, these birds are more intelligent than a lot of people think. We always have house martins building here in the summer and, of course, plenty of pigeons and seagulls.

I think for anyone when they reach retirement to live so near to nature is the most wonderful thing on earth. We are lucky to be living in the middle of a fifteen acre field and after leading a busy life as my wife and myself have done I feel it is as near to heaven on earth as anyone could get. When I look around I very often think our living has not been in vain.

I have had my leg pulled quite often about the size of our family I always tell them 'the coal was better and so was the cylinder oil in them old days'.